Atlant

A creak, a crunching growl, a roar. A brief dazzle of light. He tried to leap for the wall, as the Coal had told him to do, but his bad ankle gave way.

The roof fell in.

In rocky caverns deep below the Antarctic ice lies the new kingdom of Atlantis. The Atlantans have lived there for centuries, safe from the cold and darkness Outside and watched over by their Gods. Until one day, a boy called Mungith decides to take his trial for Adulthood by working in the old coal mines, shoring up the crumbling roofs. What he discovers there puts the whole of Atlantis in danger and could bring their ordered and peaceful existence to an end.

FRANCES MARY HENDRY was a teacher in Scotland for over twenty years. She has also run a small guest house which only had visitors in the summer, which meant she could write all winter. Until 1986, when she won the S. A. C. Literary Award for her book *Quest for Kelpie*, the only writing she had done was pantomimes for her local drama club— something she still enjoys doing. She also won the S. A. C. Literary Award for *Quest for a Maid* in 1988 and has had five other books published since then. *Atlantis* is her second book for Oxford University Press.

Her other interests include history (until men started to wear trousers), gardening, embroidery, and amateur dramatics—especially pantomimes.

Chandra

ISBN 0 19 271712 X

Winner of the Writer's Guild Award and the Lancashire Book Award

Aged eleven, Chandra set out for her arranged marriage full of hope and happiness. But out in the desert, far from home, the realization of her future begins to dawn on her. Somehow she must keep her own identity—but how?

'This is an incredibly moving book, which is highly recommended.'

Books for Keeps

'Not only a gripping tale, but a valuable reminder that tradition still everywhere holds its power.' *The Observer*

Atlantis

Other books by Frances Mary Hendry

Quest for a Kelpie
Quest for a Maid
Quest for a Babe
Quest for a Queen—1. *The Lark*
2. *The Falcon*   3. *The Jackdaw*
Jenny
The Seer's Stone
Chandra

Atlantis

Frances Mary Hendry

Oxford University Press
Oxford New York Toronto

Oxford University Press, Great Clarendon Street, Oxford
OX2 6DP

Oxford New York
Athens Auckland Bangkok Bogota Bombay
Buenos Aires Calcutta Cape Town Dar es Salaam
Delhi Florence Hong Kong Istanbul Karachi
Kuala Lumpur Madras Madrid Melbourne
Mexico City Nairobi Paris Singapore
Taipei Tokyo Toronto

and associated companies in
Berlin Ibadan

Oxford is a trade mark of Oxford University Press

Copyright © Frances Mary Hendry 1997
First published 1997

The author has asserted her moral right to be
known as the author of the work.

A CIP catalogue record for this book is available
from the British Library

ISBN 0 19 271751 0

Cover design by Slatter Anderson
Cover illustration by Kevin Jenkins

Printed and bound in Great Britain by
Biddles Ltd, Guildford and King's Lynn

In the beginning,
in the white tides ...

Rassiyyak, the Great God of Fire,
Osiriyyak, the Great God of Rock,
and **Issiyyal**, the Great Goddess of Water,
made the world,
and it was called **Atlantis**.
And they made people, to make it more interesting.
To watch the people, **Rassiyyak** flew across
the roof of the world,
higher than sixty birds could fly,
and gave warmth and light to the whole world for a tide,
and then he dived under the rock, and for the next tide
it was black and dark and cold.
But after sixty times sixty times sixty cycles of years,
Rassiyyak saw that the people forgot the great gods.
The great gods were angered.
So **Rassiyyak** flew high and low in the sky,
and all was cold and dark, or burning and blinding
and **Osiriyyak** sent earthquakes and volcanoes
and **Issiyyal** sent tidal waves and floods
and all the world died.

But a young man and a young woman,
Rammesak and **Elonal**,
were out in a boat, fishing with their cats.
They begged for help from two of the little gods,
Beliyyak the Dolphin God and **Bastiyyal** the Cat Goddess.
They floated for sixty tides.
Dolphins led them, and they found dodos and cavies and rats,
and a cockroach hid under their nets.
At last the little gods led them to the centre of the
world,
where they found a huge cavern in a rock,
and the roof fell behind to hide them from the great gods.
There was light glowing all around, and warmth, and food.
Outside was cold and darkness and hunger and madness and
death.
So **Rammesak** and **Elonal** stayed where they were safe,
and dug houses for themselves and their children.
And they spoke to the little gods, **Beliyyak** and **Bastiyyal**,
saying
'Thank you for leading us to this safe shelter.
Please live with us and watch over us, but not too closely.'
So **Rammesak** and **Elonal** were the first Father and Mother
of the people of the new world of
Atlantis.

Atlantis

Atlantis is a huge complex of many caves underneath Antarctica, on the edge of the volcanic field which surfaces in the volcano of Mount Erebus. The nearby lava melts ice from the glaciers above for water. The tide enters through underwater tunnels and holes at each end of the chain of caverns, in spouts and whirlpools. Rising, it forces stale air out under the edges of the ice, and sucks fresh, cold air in as it falls. The people know only one way out, which they call Death Gate.

A luminous film of algae covers everything, giving enough light for their large eyes to see by. In addition, a few caves have holes up to the ice above, where dim sunlight filters through. These caves are used for breeding cavies, dodos, and rats, and for growing lichens. Lava holes are utilized as foundries and smithies for copper, bronze, and glass, and coal is mined. Many kinds of resins are produced. Shellfish and seaweeds, eels and octopus are farmed, and seals use these wide caves as a resting-place in winter. Friendly dolphins enjoy hauling boats for the Wave Family, for a reward of fish. The deep water of the main caverns provides fish, sharks, and sea mammals. Huge, dangerous wild rats scavenge round the City.

Time is measured by the tides. A day is two tides (about 25 hours), called light-tide and dark-tide—a memory of Outside. About half the people are awake during each tide, and at change-over at high-tides there is a general meeting time of about four hours, when they have their main meals—light-dinner and dark-dinner. They count in sixties, not hundreds; $60 = 3 \times 4 \times 5$. An Atlantan year is six sixty-days; actually 375 days, in the Outside world. So a cycle is the time it takes for the longest day Outside to go ahead, over the years, and return to the same date; about 36 years. Nobody worries very much; with little light, there is little use for writing and records. History becomes legend; what is forgotten, they say, is not worth remembering.

Atlantis holds about 8,000 people. They are small, mostly about 1.2m, tough and wiry, with large, sensitive eyes. Several have mental powers—telepathy, healing, finding, etc. Children pass a Trial to gain the rights and duties of an Adult, and may choose to do so at any time after puberty. Then, before they marry, most become Hunters for two or three years, to gain teeth of, for example, rat, shark, or dolphin, which are Atlantan money.

The Families of Atlantis live in Houses dug out of the soft pumice cliffs round the main City cavern. The bigger, richer, better-run Families live in the three lower terraces above the harbour. The ever-changing Roof Houses, mostly small— Kelp is the biggest—burrow and squabble above them and in a few smaller off-shoot caves. A husband joins the House of his wife. People can change House by being adopted, at any age, into any House which will accept them. The Council of all the Fathers and Mothers, the heads of the 160-plus Families, decides all matters of Custom, which is their law. It is led by a King and Queen chosen by the Council. They are the judges and advisers to the Families, and as the embodiments of Atlantis must sacrifice themselves to the Little Gods in any grave disaster.

The Atlantans believe in reincarnation, so, although they mourn the loss of a friend or relation, death doesn't worry them much. Any baby that its House Mother judges will be a drag or a danger to its Family is sent back to the Gods at once, for better luck next life.

Rogues who repeatedly break Custom or Manners are cast out of the Families to become Wilders, who live in lawless, brutal squalor in an off-shoot cave system; no one else goes in. They can earn teeth for trade by doing the heavy, dirty work, like clearing blocked drains or shovelling clinker from the lava furnaces. People judged too troublesome or violent are thrust out of Death Gate to the deadly cold of Outside, from where souls cannot return.

Point House is one of the largest Houses, a Second Level Family, an off-shoot of Copper and Coal. Its mark is a tall chevron in copper and black, and its speciality is heavy or quality bronze-work—spears, knives, anchors. Its own off-shoot Families are all named Triangles, and mainly make small metal goods—buckles, hinges, etc. Points tend to be tall and strong.

Point Mother, Feelissal, married twice. When her grand-uncle retired as Point Father both her husbands claimed the position, but the Family insisted on choosing her son Distomak, her only child by her first husband. Point Mother has three daughters: Prentastal, calm and strong, the tallest person in Atlantis at 1m 60cm; Motoral, who loves the big hunting cats bred by Cat Family; and Chooker, small and lively. Chooker is about twelve Atlantan years old. She is a light-tide person, like Point Mother, and so is her older cousin Mungith, son of Point Mother's sister.

THE GODS OF ATLANTIS ARE:

Rassiyyak, GREAT God of FIRE

Osiriyyak, GREAT God of Rock

Issiyyal, GREAT Goddess of WATER

Beliyyak, Dolphin God of men

Bastiyyal, CAT Goddess of women

THE MAIN PEOPLE OF ATLANTIS WHO APPEAR IN THIS BOOK ARE:

POINT HOUSE: **Feelissal**, POINT MoTher;

her son **Distomak**, POINT FaTher;

her daughters **Prentastal, Motoral, Chooker**;

her sister's son **Mungith**.

DROP HOUSE: **Crosstenak**   COAL HOUSE: **Giffaral**

KELP HOUSE: **King Pyroonak**; his sister **Hemomnal**

GRANITE HOUSE: **Queen Sullival**

RATS: **Peepik**, Chooker's pet, **Meelin**, Mungith's pet,

Veenik, POINT MoTher's messenger.

THE FIRST LEVEL FAMILIES ARE:
Granite, Pearl, Coal, Tooth, Gold, Copper, Cavy, Fish, Fire, Yeast, Ice.

THE SECOND LEVEL FAMILIES ARE:
Point, Glass, Boat, Dodo, Block, Crystal, Silver, Shark, Harpoon, Wave, Bowl, Rope, Weave, Rat.

THE THIRD LEVEL FAMILIES ARE:
Dot, Drop, Spiral, Chain, Swirl, Square, Rectangle, Pentagon, Hexagon, Octagon, Ring, Chain, Check, Key, Cross, Saltire, Vertical Stripe, Horizontal Stripe, Slash, Perpendicular, Oval, 4 Stars, 2 Diamonds, Eel, Bird, Arrow, Loop, Heart, 6 Triangles, Hook, Shell, Fan.

The Roof Families are mostly small and irregular;
they constantly grow and fail, split and merge.
They are mostly named after objects or animals, e.g. Kelp, Tube, Hand, Gel, Lace.

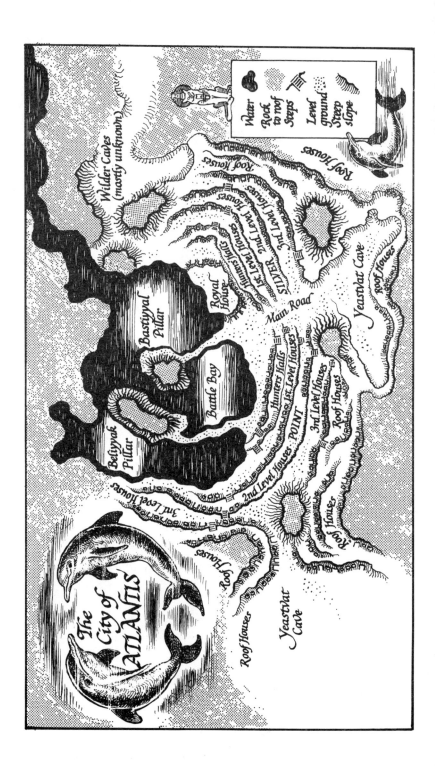

1

'Mung, we'll be late! Think if we missed the first kill! Your hair must be set by now! Hurry up! They might even have started!' Chooker was yelling urgently. She stood on tiptoe to peer down over the flat roof of Pearl House, on the First Level directly below Point, but it was crowded with Pearls eager to watch the Battle from their grandstand position. She could barely see the God signs on the harbour pillars, let alone the boats.

The Nurses on duty were settling the toddlers and oldsters of Point House up on the roof above her already, with drinks and snacks, stools and rugs for comfort. For a moment, Chooker wondered if she might not be better off up there— but no. The echoing buzz of the crowds jamming the quaysides filled her with excitement. 'Come on! We'll never get near the front!'

As soon as she saw the doorway curtain start to lift, she didn't wait any longer for her cousin, but launched herself down the slide beside the steps that led from Second Level down towards the harbour, slithering over the polished bumps with a happy disregard for her new codskin kilt, her long plait of black hair flying behind her. Peepik, her pet rat, clung to his pad on her shoulder, gleefully squeaking and whipping his long tail as she skidded round the curves.

Too nearly Adult to take the children's slide, Mungith raced down the steps behind her, to reach the roadway below just behind his young cousin. 'We've loads of time, silly! There are still Fathers and Mothers coming down Main Road.'

The City's central street wound up from the harbour, the only flat area in the cavern, past the old cramped cliff houses where the Hunters lived now, rising steeply past the jutting

11

rock of the Royal House, twisting through the circling terraces where the big, important Houses like Pearl and Point were dug, on and on up to the burrows near the roof, and the outer caves. It was full of stragglers hurrying down to the harbour like themselves, but two Family groups were pushing through the rush. One was dressed and painted in white and pale blue stripes, with a pink sea anemone tattooed on their shoulders, and the other in gaudy yellow, green, and purple spirals.

'Stop that, you silly dodo!' Chooker slapped at Peepik, who was wriggling in excitement. 'Oh, the Spirals and the Sea Anemones are always late. Father Spiral dithers so, he'll miss the tide for his own funeral, and Mother Sea Anemone's almost as vain as you are, Mung!'

'I am not vain!' Mungith protested. But he couldn't help putting up a careful finger to check—no, his hair was fine. His body paint was itchy, children didn't paint so he'd never done it before, but he'd get used to it. And his new kilt was sharkskin, richly embroidered in the striking copper and black chevrons of Point House. Yes, the girls would all be looking . . .

Chooker was grinning as she trotted along. 'You mean you used to be conceited, but now you're perfect? Oh, Mung!'

Annoyed, he had to get his own back. He grabbed his young cousin's arm to make her listen to him. 'Look, Chooker, will you stop calling me Mung! Mungith! If you don't mind.'

Chooker actually stopped to stare at him. 'Look, what's got into you just now?' She flipped his new necklace, a silver chain with three shark's teeth on it, which showed he was no longer a boy but a man, able to claim an Adult Trial whenever he felt ready for it. 'You're turning into a pompous bore these tides, prettifying as if you were getting married and moaning about your dignity like a Father! Stiffer than Distom!'

12

Mungith was embarrassed, but couldn't show it. He tried to stand on his dignity. 'Well, when I'm an Adult, you'll have to treat me with proper respect, so you might as well start now. Don't call me that short baby name, and so on.'

'Proper respect? You? Eh, I know you too well!' she jeered. She loved him, she was going to marry him when she grew up, but if she showed it his hair would puff up to twice the size. 'Oh, come on! Or we'll never see a thing.'

He turned after her, his longer legs taking steady strides beside her trotting short ones.

Naturally, the whole of the City had come down to the harbour, rushing dark-dinner to watch the Battle. Points tended to breed large, though, and Mungith was already bigger and heavier than many Hunters. His sturdy weight pushed and wriggled a path for them both until they got stuck beside a stone shed not far from the quay; a new storage shed, built, not dug out like a proper house.

'I knew it!' Chooker grumbled. 'You and your fancy hair! I can't see a thing down here! Ouch!' Peepik was getting frightened in the crush, and trying to climb on top of her head.

'You shouldn't have brought him!' If Mungith stood on tiptoe he could see the boats, but little Chook was lost among people's chests. Behind them a couple of Wilders were edging closer. He might lose his necklace, with his three precious teeth—why had he worn it? Trying to show off—but nobody could see him in this crowd . . . Where could they go?

He looked up. The roof above them was loaded with Hunters. They were often a bit rough. But it couldn't be worse than down here. His hair was getting knocked askew; that decided him. 'Hey! Any room up there?' he called.

Faces looked down between the dangling feet. 'For you or your girl?' somebody yelled.

A woman laughed. 'Hey, Mungith! And Chooker!'

It was his cousin, Chooker's eldest sister. 'Hey, Prentastal!' he called in relief.

'Hunch over, you lot!' she called, shoving her friends along. 'They're my Family! Toss your rat up, Chook! Give me a hand, Crossten.'

A man beside her grinned and reached down, his shark-tooth necklace and armlets clattering. 'Come on then, bonny boy! Give the girl a lift up—and now you—up you come! Mind your fancy hair-do!' Hard, strong hands easily hauled the youngsters up to the flat roof.

'You stand at the back. We can't see past that hair, bonny boy!' they laughed, but Mungith didn't mind. Wilders would just have mashed his hair flat, and kicked him off the roof if he complained. But then, Wilders wouldn't have lifted them, even if he'd dared ask them to. And up here, he could see well—and everybody could see him.

Chooker got a good seat, right on the front edge beside her sister. Peepik was leaping about on her sister's knee, licking her face, the copper glitter on his long tail and whiskers sparkling with his joy. 'See, he remembers you! Calm down, you silly, or you'll fall and a Wilder'll have you for dinner! How are you, Prentast? Prentastal, I mean! I like the new kilts!'

'Showy, aren't they?' Her big sister preened and smoothed the fine black-and-white hide. While young Adults were Hunters, winning a dowry of teeth, their comrades were their Family and they dropped their House colours. 'Killer whale, of course. Enough skin for kilts for us all.'

'You're a matching set! Smart!' Chooker was impressed. 'Did you harpoon it yourself?'

'No, I'm just a paddler. Our harpooner's Crosstenak here.' Prentast grinned at the sturdy, cheery-faced man by her side. 'But I got ten teeth!'

'Marvellous!' Chooker said in admiration. 'When are you coming home?'

'Oh, when I've got enough teeth to get married on! Nearly there!' her sister boasted, tapping the wealth of seal, shark, and dolphin teeth proudly displayed in clicketing tassels round her neck and chest, arms and calves. 'Tell Mother I'll be home soon, Beliyyak willing.'

'Eh, this is wonderful, Prentast!' Chook was quivering with excitement. 'The buzz of the crowd—I can hear it, right through my head!' She wasn't a strong Senser, but the crowd's emotions were intense. 'I feel I could fly! Thank you for lifting us!'

2

Everything within the immense cavern was luminous, from the high vault of the roof glowing above, down the shining terraces of Houses, to the gleaming skins of the crowd packed round the harbour. The fresh green and purple paint on the battered old boats chosen for the Battle shone brightly against the silver shimmer of Battle Bay, the centre harbour basin. Here and there a triangular fin cut a long black ripple. Sharks always knew when there would be food.

The two Families were lined along the piers. Battle Custom banned all armour, even gloves or mining helmets. Their young Hunters shouted insults across at each other, waved bows and harpoons, juggled spears and axes, showing off. The oldsters handled their spears and clubs with desperate determination; it was a long time since they'd been Hunters. But by Custom, all Adults from each Family must take part.

'Doesn't Father Kelp look old? How many have to die?' Chooker asked.

'About a quarter of each House!' Prentastal nodded grimly. 'Yes, you may well gasp! The sharks'll feed well this tide. Dot House is very narrow, so they dug back seven rows deep, and found they couldn't ventilate so far in. They had to use the back three rows just for storage. Kelp House is directly above them, and the stupid cavies let it get far too crowded, so they broke down into Dot House and walled off three rear rooms— they could get fresh air in from above. You know how rough Kelps are, they'd never dream of asking, and renting rooms. When the Dots found out, did you know they were actually fighting in the tunnels?'

Chooker nodded. 'We heard. Hitting each other like Wilders. Not proper duels at all.'

'That's right. It could have been settled in Council, but somebody hit somebody else, and it spread. Disgusting! So now the numbers have to come right down, or it'll all start over.' Prentastal shook her head angrily. 'If I was Queen, I'd throw both Mothers out of Death Gate for sheer carelessness. Those younger Families up near the Roof—they're sloppy.'

'Watch it!' Crosstenak protested. 'I'm from one of "those younger Families", you snob!'

'Drops aren't a Roof Family!' She grinned at him. 'You know what I mean. Half their Mothers don't do their job. They don't insist on Manners, or proper birth control, or even clean their yeast-vats properly. And when the Houses are small, only two or three rooms, and you have too many people jammed in, always half drunk or poisoned, with no proper Manners, they get used to squabbling, and then the whole City has trouble. It's dangerous. We don't need it.'

Chooker sensed an extra worry in Prentastal's mind. 'Why specially not now?'

Prentastal glanced at her sideways. 'Are you reading me? Well. . . Leave it till later, cockle. Listen, there's the clapping, the King and Queen are coming. And there's the Priest with the trumpet. Hold Peepik's collar, cockle, or he'll jump off in fright. It's starting.'

The flowing white tunics of King Pyroonak and Queen Sullival glowed bright against the rich brilliance of the massed Mothers and Fathers behind them, as they settled on to their benches. The Priest of the Little Gods lifted his ancient conch shell, and the deep, echoing moan silenced the applause of the crowd. Only the silver ripple on the boats and quay walls broke the silence, and the dark swish of fins and tails.

At the ends of the twin piers, the huge rock pillars that helped hold up the cavern roof were carved and painted with the symbols of the Little Gods. The hot Dolphin, who lived in the roaring cold and dark of the whirlpools where the tides

17

rose and fell, was the God for men, and the young King rose and turned towards his leaping red curve. 'Beliyyak, hear us!' he called. His voice hadn't yet lost the piercing, carrying shrillness that all Hunters developed. He had only been King for a few sixty-tides, chosen for enormous bravery in saving a boat-load of his mates from an underwater lava blast just before the old King died.

'Beliyyak, hear us!' The crowd roared the call after him. 'I hear!' echoed from the steep far wall and the deep hollows of the furthest caves.

The white circle on the other pillar was the sign of the cold Cat Goddess, who lived in the lava flows that warmed Atlantis and dangerously fuelled the foundries and smithies. Queen Sullival called to the Goddess, more softly, 'Bastiyyal! Hear us!'

'Bastiyyal, hear us!' everyone shouted.

Again, the echoes replied, 'I hear!'

The crowd clapped gently, murmuring, 'The Gods hear us!' They didn't usually pay much attention, thankfully. But on an exciting occasion like this they'd be watching with interest.

'Two Families are here.' The King gestured to the line of men and women dressed and painted in luminous green and gold, on his side of the harbour. 'The Kelps.'

On the Queen's side, rather more glowed purple, blue, and crimson. She pointed to them. 'The Dots.'

'Eight Kelps must die.' The King's voice was strained. The crowd sighed in compassion. Pyroonak was a Kelp. It would be hard for him to watch his own Family fight, and not help.

'Twelve Dots must die.' The old Queen was upset, too. She was a Granite, one of the First Level Families, and wasn't personally involved, but she was kindly and gentle.

On bollards on the quay, the Priest set out two trays with stones to mark the number who must be killed before the Battle could end.

The King and Queen reached out to the Gods' pillars.

'Beliyyak, let the Battle be fought fast and fair.'

'Bastiyyal, let no one be a coward, to shame Atlantis, nor crippled, to burden Atlantis.'

They turned to each other, and spoke together. 'For the good of Atlantis.'

'For the good of Atlantis.' The crowd repeated it. The older people were sombre, but the youngsters were already squealing with excitement.

Grimly, the two Families boarded their boats. 'Look, there's Hemmin,' Prentastal commented. 'The King's older sister. The one with the big axe. She's a Wilder—a real sharp flint! The Dots had her thrown out years ago for bullying. We chased her only ten tides back, when she tried to steal ropes from our boat. She hopes the Kelps will take her back if she fights well for them.'

At the back, Mungith had been posing with casual art, carefully ignoring two pretty Pearl girls who were standing on their roof blowing kisses to him and giggling. A horrid suspicion was growing in him. They couldn't be laughing at him—could they? He checked—his hair had been knocked squint! Oh, no! He scarcely noticed as the traditional stamping and clapping started, slow at first, feet thudding on rock, tooth anklets and bracelets rattling, settling into a steady beat that would grow faster and faster to drive on the fighters and cover the screams.

Chook's heart swelled with terror and thrill. This was her first Battle. What would it be like? She could scarcely breathe.

The mournful hoot of the Priest's conch shell loosed the Families into Battle.

Instantly, in a planned move, the Dot Hunters sent a shower of shark-tooth arrows into the packed Kelp boats.

Mungith, still worrying about his hair, jumped at the roar of applause and screams.

The dead were tipped overboard into a swirl of sharks, and

the Priest tossed three green-painted stones into the harbour.

The boats rowed closer, the Kelps urgent to kill their quota of Dots before too many of their own died. Arrows and harpoons flew, the boats bumped, people grabbed and shoved, swung and stabbed. More stones splashed into the harbour.

The deep stamping drum-beat echoed deafeningly under the vault till the cormorants and petrels who lived in the rocky roof swooped screaming in alarm above the fight.

The priest had only two green stones left, but seven purple ones, when the biggest Kelp boat heaved away to one side. 'Cowards!' yelled Mungith, finally forgetting about his hair.

'Watch!' Crosstenak shouted over the din. 'Hemmin's in it!'

The tall woman at the tiller shouted to her paddlers, and the Kelp boat charged forward. Its bow crashed over the side of a Dot boat, and bore it down. The water swirled silver, black, and red as sharks frenzied for their food, while the Kelps swung axes and clubs at the heads and hands that tried to climb aboard their boat, and drew off to try again.

'Three!' Crosstenak yelled. 'Evens it up a bit, eh? Hemmin's idea, I'll swear!'

'Mother Dot's gone,' Prentastal commented. 'And Father Kelp. They'll maybe get better ones now. Eh, Junnif's hurt—but she's got him—well done, Junnif!'

Crosstenak grinned. 'You owe me ten teeth—Fraltik's gone.'

'Learn to count! Norteez got two Kelps, at six each, so you owe me two!' Prentastal was jubilant. 'Ay, he's got another. That's eight you owe me!'

Chooker couldn't join in the glee. Everybody gambled on anything, of course, and normally she'd have been cheering her sister's win, but not now. She felt ill. She hadn't expected it to be like this. 'There's the last Kelp stones gone. Will they stop now?'

'Not yet,' Prentastal told her. 'Not till the Dots have lost another two—no, just one now. Not long, cockle, and it'll be all over.'

Another two Kelps died before Hemmin's axe sent the last Dot stone splashing into the harbour and the Priest sounded the final blast on his conch shell, to allow the fighters to stop.

By Custom, no one could leave until the last of the wounded had had their wounds tended, and been carried home. Even though the Silvers and Hearts, the small Families who specialized in medicine and surgery, and Nurses from many Families came to help, it took a much longer time than Chooker wanted. She couldn't help starting to cry. As the crowd's excitement faded, the Families' grief and pain could reach her mind.

Prentastal nodded sympathetically. 'Yes, it's shocking, the first time you see someone hurt. Hunters get used to it, fairly well, but a Battle's far, far worse.'

Sniffing, Chook leaned against the comforting, tough warmth of her big sister. 'I knew, that is I'd been told, but it's different when you see it. That's the idea, I suppose. You'll never let our Family get into this kind of thing, will you, when you're Point Mother?'

Prentastal grinned. 'I can promise you that, cockle! The Kelps have taken Hemmin back. It's a mistake—she'll cause them more trouble, she can't help it. She's Hemminal again, now—and if you meet her, be sure to use her full name, cockle, she'll be touchy about it. Oh, well. Look, that's the last one going up now. Now the King and Queen can leave, and then all the rest of us. Good, I'm starving!'

'You always are.' Crosstenak leaned over, holding out a small bag. 'Here. Smoked mussels, with a new spice the Spider Crabs have grown. It's good.'

'Ay, you're wonderful!' Prentastal grabbed the treat. 'M'm! Have one, Chook? Go on, you'll feel better, half your trouble's just emptiness. Mungith?'

'Thanks,' Mungith smiled, taking a couple of the titbits. His knees were trembling. Hunters were used to this? It would be a while yet, he thought, before he'd claim Adulthood. Or was that cowardice? No, his sickness was because he wanted to go home, away from those giggling Pearl girls, nothing to do with the Battle.

3

Soon after dark-dinner only four tides later, Chooker was at lessons with the other children, chanting the Song of the Rebirth of Osiriyyak, when she was called to speak to her mother, as Feelissal, Point Mother.

If it was normal mother-daughter business, Feelissal would simply stick her head out into the Hall, where no one slept, and yell, 'Eh! Chooker! Chook! Come to mother!' and the word would be passed along. But this time her messenger rat, Veenik, trotted in from the Office with a formal message to the Teacher in the bone basket strapped to his back.

'Chooker, Point Mother wishes to speak to you.' The old Teacher raised an eyebrow at her. 'On you go, you don't keep a Mother waiting.'

Chooker gulped. She hadn't done anything terribly bad. Had she? Politely touching her forefingers to her chest and bowing to the Teacher, she hurried after Veenik.

Frisking along, the knee-high rat suddenly pounced on a flicker along the foot of the wall; a cockroach, long as his head! 'Good boy, Veenik!' Chooker cheered up. A good sign!

The heavy felt door curtain of the Office was down; Mother had a visitor. Her voice was raised loud enough to be heard. Oh, dear! Best Manners, if Mother was annoyed! Nervously, Chooker smoothed her hair and kilt. Lucky it was clean . . .

When she tapped the chiming shells by the door, the scolding stopped. 'Come!' Chooker lifted the curtain aside, followed Veenik in and bowed formally, fingers to chest.

Prentastal was sitting on a visitors' padded stool, wearing her fine black and white kilt and all her wealth of teeth. Chooker smiled and bowed to her sister, but Prentastal just raised her eyebrows in resigned silence as Mother glared at her.

Veenik had scampered up to Mother's chair to be petted. 'What's that he's eating?' Mother demanded. 'Eh, disgusting! Yes, yes, well done, Veenik! Now go to bed, good boy! And don't drop any legs off it!' Squeaking happily, Veenik took the remains of his catch to crunch noisily in his basket.

Frowning, Mother turned to Chooker, who hastily straightened her face. 'Chooker, do you know what your sister has been saying to me? Well? Do you? Speak up!'

'She's going to come home?' Chooker offered hopefully.

'Huh! If that was all of it!' Mother snorted. 'She's going to get married!'

'Oh, good!' Chooker was delighted. 'It'll be wonderful to have you home again, Prentast, and we've a free yeast-vat so you won't need to wait to get married. Who have you chosen? Uncle Billit? Or Voster, he's handsome, and he's quite a strong Senser, he'd be a good Father.'

She was surprised to see her sister making a resigned face, while Mother replied. 'Who? A good question. But not a good answer! A man from her own House isn't good enough for her. She has to go outside for a husband—and not even to one of the Founding Families. A Drop. A nobody from the Third Level! A Drop!' She stopped, apparently unable to go on for emotion.

'You know him, Chook.' Prentastal didn't seem as scared by Mother's outburst as Chooker expected. She was even smiling gently. 'At the Battle—Crosstenak. Remember?'

'Oh, yes. He's very nice.' Chooker was trying to take it in.

'Ayy! You know this man? You've met him? I suppose I should be glad that at least somebody in the House has met my First Daughter's future husband!' Mother almost screamed.

Something came to Chooker's mind, so important that she couldn't keep it in. 'But if you don't marry someone from your own House, Prentast, you can't be the next Mother.'

'Ayy! She's realized it! Even the little sister realizes it! And

24

did the older one realize it? Did she?' Mother was waving her arms about, sobbing wildly, tugging as if she was demented at the strings of copper beads plaited into her hair. She must be very upset, Chooker thought. She wasn't usually as emotional as this. It was rather frightening.

Prentastal just smiled. 'Of course, Mother,' she stated calmly. 'I knew it perfectly well. I told you. Six years ago, I told you I didn't want to be Point Mother, running the House, deciding which babies we adopt out or keep or send to the Little Gods, and everybody running to me for help and advice—all the responsibility, the arguments, the pressure—yay, never! You said I'd change my mind, I didn't know what I was talking about, it wasn't up to me to make the decision anyway. You'd not listen, so I didn't argue. It wasn't worth the upset. Anything might have happened. I could have been killed in a hunt. I might never have found anyone I liked well enough to marry. I might have changed my mind. But I didn't. And of course I knew a woman who marries outside her House can never be Mother of that House. Why do you think I'm doing it? Let alone that I like Crossten better than any man I've ever met.'

'Eh, Bastiyya! Such a daughter! A tooth in my heart!' Mother sank down into her big chair, hiding her face in her hands. 'Is he at least useful?' she sobbed. 'After he leaves the Hunters' Halls, to come and join you here, what will he do? What are the Drops good at—glasswork? But our furnaces are for metal, not glass!'

'His father was a Crystal, Mother. He's got an idea for making lights with our wires and glass gems from the Drops. It's beautiful. Give us five years, and this House will glitter.'

Mother's sobs stopped as if a curtain had dropped. There was a long pause.

One of Prentastal's eyelids winked gently, where only Chooker could see. Chooker hid a smile. Prentast was clever; Mother always wanted new finery for her House.

At last, Mother raised her hands theatrically. 'Well. What can a poor woman do, when her own children ignore her wishes, disregard her advice, destroy her hopes?'

Shaking her head, she turned to look at Chooker.

Chooker's heart seemed to lurch inside her. It couldn't be true!

'So now you, my youngest daughter. I turn to you. You will not forsake me, I know.'

Yes, it was true! Chooker gasped for breath. She was being chosen as First Daughter, Mother's heir, to be next Point Mother!

'You're bright, and you work hard when you put your mind to it. You're a slight Senser—a House doesn't like a lot, but a little is a real asset for a Mother. You can keep secrets—yes, I know how often you covered for that rascal Mungith! You'll do very well.'

Chooker finally managed to draw a breath. 'But what about Motoral?'

Her Mother sniffed. 'Don't be a fool, or I'll think I've chosen wrongly again! Your older sister is not fit to be a Family Mother. Not even in a Roof House!'

Prentast was nodding. 'I know she's a Hunter already, Chooker, but even if her temper was less explosive, she cares for absolutely nothing except her hunting cats.'

Mother sniffed. 'Motor is thinking of asking Cat House to adopt her, anyway. No. We need a definite heir. Now.' She and Prentast nodded grimly to each other. Again, Chooker got the drift of a thought: *Especially just now* . . .

'It's you, my sweet little cockle. You're the only one!' Prentastal suddenly picked Chooker up, hugging her fiercely. 'And I wish you all the luck in the world!'

On a rack of carved sharkbone at the side of the room hung the gorgeous copper and jet ceremonial jewellery of Point Mother, the crown with its high peak at the back and the deep-fringed ear-chain, the foot-wide anklets, bracelets, and necklace. Below hung the First Daughter's pendant, which Prentastal had left there for safety when she joined the Hunters' Halls.

With formality, Mother took it down. 'My First Daughter Chooker, wear this with honour and good sense, and my crown after it.' She settled the chain on Chooker's neck, so that the glittering copper and jet chevron hung on her chest.

'Congratulations, Chook,' Prentastal said, smiling.

'But . . . but—' Overwhelmed, Chooker couldn't think, couldn't move, couldn't breathe.

'But nothing!' Mother said firmly. 'Unless you're going to argue, too! No? Then be quiet. There are serious matters that the First Daughter needs to know about.'

'Yes, Mother.' It was always safe to say that. Stunned, Chooker sank on to the stool that Mother pointed to—a padded stool, not a plain one, because of her new rank. She couldn't help touching the pendant. It meant so much—it meant—

She jumped as Mother snapped, 'Pay attention, Chooker!'

Chooker suddenly realized that Mother's upset had all been acting. Well, mostly. Mother had to make sure that Prentastal actually did mean what she said—and she enjoyed a bit of drama. Now, though, the hysterics had vanished.

From a shelf, Mother took down a long, pointed metal object. 'Look at that. What do you think of it?'

Chooker took it gingerly. 'It's a spear-head, isn't it?'

Prentastal nodded. 'That's right. But it's not ours. I brought it up to check with Distom and the Smiths. It was stuck in the side of a shark that we killed two sixty-tides ago. The edge never seems to get nicked or blunted, better than our best bronze. We've found three others like it. For three cycles we've been finding stuff in sharks and whales and seals— harpoon heads and little balls, deep in the flesh. And lately, in their stomachs, there have been bits of net and rope you

27

just can't break, and bottles and things we don't understand, in stuff like hardset gel, but not quite the same.'

Chooker sensed what her sister meant. 'You think it came from Outside? But nobody can live there! Nobody could survive Outside, in the cold and white and black, right under the eye of Rassiyyak!'

Prentastal shook her head. 'Apparently somebody does. Or some thing.'

There was a long silence, while Chooker tried to accept the idea. Mother was nodding. 'There's more, feather. You remember my older brother Whectorak?'

Prentastal nodded. 'He married into Granite House, didn't he?'

'Yes. They work up in the furthest marble quarry, the new one they're opening at the end of Three Pinks Cave. Just four tides ago he told me that for almost a year they've been hearing noises—deep bangs and cracks in the rock, and a heavy grinding, not the normal shifting of the rocks or the ice above. They were so worried, they called in the Priest to see if the lava or the ice were moving, but he says there's no feeling of pressure there at all. But . . .'

'The sounds could have come from Outside.' Prentastal looked grim.

'I've heard nothing, in Council or casually.' Mother started to pace up and down the room. 'Nor has Distom. He'd have said, if any of the other Fathers had mentioned it. Or were worried about it—you know how good a Senser he is, he'd have picked it up.'

'Well, will you try to find out, Mother? Maybe there are other signs, but everyone's trying to keep them quiet, to avoid panic. Or because they just can't believe it. I scarcely can, myself. But we must find out, and then decide what they mean, and what we're going to do about it.'

Mother sighed. 'You'd be such a good Mother. Ay, well.' She considered for a moment. 'I'll go visiting, chat with my friends, see what I can discover without fussing the Council. Yes. And I have a perfect reason.' She glanced at Chooker. 'My new First Daughter needs to meet all the Mothers, and their First Daughters. You'll be working together later on, in the Council.'

Prentastal laughed at Chooker's worried face. 'Don't be scared, cockle! They don't bite.' She rose to go, and bowed courteously to Mother. 'I'll bring Crosstenak tomorrow, Mother, and introduce him to you and the Family at dinner. If that will suit?'

Mother returned the formal bow. 'You and your husband-to-be will be welcome.'

Chooker rose, too. 'Mother . . . may I go?' She felt as if she was smothering in the deepest store-rooms where the air never changed.

Her mother—not Point Mother—gave her a big hug. 'You'll move into the First Daughter's cubicle tomorrow, feather. It'll be a change for you, having a place all to yourself.' She paused for a moment, considering. 'Who's your dark-tide mate—Brenlym? Yes. Little Trak can move in—he's walking quite well, it's time he moved into the Nursery and left his parents in peace, and Brenlym's sensible enough to be his older sister now.' Mother smiled at Chooker's face. 'A Mother has to plan everything in her House. Prentast and her man will take a cubicle in the Married Rooms with the other families.' She sighed briefly, and sniffed. Prentastal just grinned.

'It's a shock, I know, my downy little feather, but exciting, too, isn't it?' Mother waited until Chooker nodded. Then, chuckling, she tapped the pendant. 'Off you go now, and see what everyone has to say about that!'

Outside, Prentastal hugged Chooker, too. 'I don't know whether to congratulate you, cockle, or say I'm sorry for dropping you in it!' She grinned, and then sobered. 'But listen—if you have any trouble, let me know.'

Chooker was scarcely listening. Now that she was out of Mother's sight, she was feeling the pendant, running thrilled fingers over the smooth polished stones. 'No, it'll be all right. She'll be furious, till she realizes she'd have no time for her cats if she was Mother,' she said absently.

Prentastal smiled. 'You knew I was thinking about Motor.'

Chooker looked surprised. 'Yes, of course...oh. You didn't say.'

'No.' Prentastal hugged her little sister again. 'But you sensed it. You'll make a good Mother. Now run along and tell everybody!'

Chooker danced off down the corridor. What would Mungith say?

4

Mungith congratulated her, of course; but he turned rather quiet, and when the other light-tide children—and adults, as the news spread—crowded round to chatter, he went up to perch on the edge of the roof alone, staring out over the City. He couldn't go to his cubicle, his dark-tide partner would have his hammock slung already, and you could never get away from other people in the crowded halls of the House, but by Custom nobody would disturb you if you came out here.

Chooker was going to be the next Point Mother.

His little cousin would run one of the biggest and finest Houses in Atlantis. Point's great smithies, down by the lava flows, had forged the spears which had given the Family its name in the First Tides, and still made all the quality and heavy metal-work for Atlantis. Chooker would be in charge of all the internal affairs of nearly two hundred people, with fourteen rooms dug four rows deep, fifty-nine yeast-vats, and space to build more. She would also have strong influence among the six Triangle Houses in the next Level up, offshoots of Point over the cycles, and in their offshoots in turn among the Roof Houses. She would be one of the most important Mothers in the City Council.

It was hard to take in. No, he wasn't jealous—of course not!

He suddenly started to feel better.

Even before he heard a mild cough behind him Mungith knew that Point Father, Chooker's half-brother Distomak, was there. Mungith turned his head and smiled a welcome.

The tiny man drifted over gently, as he did everything. He had never been a Hunter, never earned a wealth of teeth, but

31

everyone respected him. As a toddler he couldn't join the rough-and-tumble of normal Nursery play, in case his neck was damaged by a jerk of his huge, heavy skull; but he was such a strong Senser that he could always turn boisterous games away from himself, or move out of range in plenty of time. Distom couldn't read their minds, not unless he was touching them or they were thinking at him, trying to reach him, or unless he took the dangerous drugs that could increase his power; but he had the art of understanding them, feeling and influencing their moods, helping and advising so sweetly and wisely that no one could take offence. He spread happiness all round him, and was the most loved person in the Family.

That was why, when the old Point Father had retired three years before, the Family had rejected claims from both of Mother's husbands and her brothers; they had insisted her son should become Point Father. He preferred being called by his short, friendly name, Distom, rather than his title, or even than his full Adult name, Distomak. He said Point Mother might like being called Mother by everybody, but he didn't feel like a father to any of the Points who towered round him.

Now, he returned Mungith's smile. 'May I sit down? Ah, that's better. I'm almost asleep. Bed soon!' He yawned and stretched as he gazed out over the City, and glanced sideways. 'Mother's just told me. Surprising, eh? Chooker as First Daughter, I mean.'

'Uhuh. And just last tide I punched her for calling me a puffer fish.' Distom frowned, puzzled. 'I was trying a new hair-style.'

'Ay, I see. Quite a sharp tongue, young Chooker has sometimes. But not spiteful. And a sensible girl. She'll be a good Mother. A slight Senser—already she feels thoughts that people are trying to hide, which is a good trick to have, and she's had no training yet.' Distom paused thoughtfully.

'She'll have every man and boy in the Family courting her now, of course.'

'What?' Mungith sat up with a jerk of consternation. In the Nursery Chook had always admired him, followed him about, shared her sweets, happily acted the shark in play hunts and not cried when the toy harpoons bruised her. She could be a nuisance, wanting to tag along when he sneaked off with the older children to forbidden rat fights down in the Wilder cave, but she'd often covered for him and helped him out of trouble. Even waiting for him before the Battle, that showed she liked him. And he quite liked her. He had even vaguely considered marrying her—some time, of course, if no one better came along... To have competition was a shock.

Distom looked innocent. 'Eh, yes. Her husband will probably be the next Point Father after me.' He paused, and offered comfort. 'It could be you, of course.'

'Do you—' Mungith had to cough— 'do you think I could?'

'Eh, I think so. Point Mother, too! Yes, indeed!' Distom smiled to encourage Mungith. 'You've good reports from your Teachers for Music, Custom, Weapons, Arithmetic, Speech-making and Legend. You're well-grown, to counter Chooker's smallness—you're almost as tall as Prentast, and she's the tallest person in Atlantis. You're quite a good-looking boy.'

Mungith, his vanity swelling at the praise, bristled slightly. Only 'quite good-looking'?

Distom hid a smile. 'Your parents were liked and respected. Fine smiths, both of them. And Krantowal was Point Mother's cousin, you're Family, so that's all right.' Krantow and Vustor had been killed by a lava blow in the smithy when Mungith was just three. Good people.

'You and Chooker are both light-tide, so you know each other well. You like her, don't you? And she likes you—and

33

that's a great deal, when a girl's choosing a husband. But there are lots of men in the running. I doubt if she'd be a second wife, but we have a score of unmarried Smiths and Hunters, with strings of teeth already to buy her presents. You'll need to work for it.'

Mungith bit a nail in sudden, unusual self-doubt. 'But I've just hit her.'

Distomak chuckled. 'You've a long time to get over that!' he soothed the lad.

'Yes.' Like Chooker earlier, Mungith was half stunned. He struggled to speak sensibly. 'I suppose there's a lot of wear in you and Point Mother yet!'

'Eh?' Distom laughed. 'Well, I actually meant that Chooker isn't even Adult yet—'

'Adult. I need to be Adult! My Trial—' Mungith jumped up. 'I'll go now—see the King—'

'Eh, calm down!' Distom was laughing so hard he had to hold his head steady. 'I'll arrange it for you. But you'll have to decide what Trial you want.' He sobered and shivered at the memory of his own. 'I wasn't strong enough for an active test, so I stayed for six tides up in the ice tunnels—my chest wouldn't have stood the choke and heat of the lava caves. I got lung fever, so it nearly killed me anyway! That wouldn't be enough for a fit youngster like you, though.'

There were lots of possible ways to prove that you were brave and strong enough to be trusted as an Adult, and people picked the one that suited them. Mungith had always said that only show-offs climbed one God Pillar, across the roof and down the next, and hunting wild rats alone, as Motoral had done, or swimming after sharks with a knife, was foolhardy. If twenty came at you at once you hadn't a chance, no matter how good you were. 'I want to do something useful. I'll go out into the old coal workings.'

'Yes.' Distom nodded. 'I thought you would—no, no, I didn't influence you at all! But to spend ten or twelve tides alone in the broken mines, shoring up crumbling roofs, with the risk of breaking a leg or getting lost or trapped by a cave-in, and dying of hunger or thirst or gas or rats—or Giants! That's a real test of control and endurance and courage. It'll be remembered.'

Mungith bit his lip. Giants? Wilders who were judged too evil to live sometimes fled to escape being put out through Death Gate. The Nurses said they wandered the lost caves and tunnels, growing huge and fierce, eating lone Miners and Hunters, and raiding Houses for disobedient, silly, violent, bad-Mannered children. Only a story, of course... but he hadn't thought about wild rats... He nodded firmly. 'That's what I want. And when I'm a Hunter, I'll win more teeth than anybody ever has!' And impress Chooker, and marry her—and maybe be Point Father some day...

Distomak might be gentle, but he was efficient. Only an hour after the next high-tide horn, long before Mungith slung his hammock, he was called to the Office. 'It's all arranged. Six tides from now. A Coal cousin will fit you with what you'll need and lead you out to an old working that needs attention. Mother says we'll hold your Adult Feast at the same time as Prentast's Wedding.' Distom smiled sweetly. 'The King is quite impressed. It's a while since any non-Miner lad went into the mines. This will make your mark. The first of many, I'm sure!'

Mungith certainly hoped so.

It was announced at the Welcome dinner for Prentastal and her husband-to-be. The Family cheered. Mungith saw the approval and admiration in everyone's eyes, especially Chooker's, and felt all smug and satisfied. Except for the idea of rats... And Giants...

5

The whole Family approved of Prentastal's man, but there was a minor problem—and Mother could put it right, and give everybody a chance to work off their excitement at the same time. She remembered only too well the size of the cockroach Veenik had caught. At the next dinner, she had an announcement for everyone. 'This House is swarming with cockroaches! And I'll not have any Drop telling his Family that Point House is bug-ridden. And as if that wasn't enough, we've seen signs of a very large rat. So I've sent to Silver House for a Doctor, and down to the Hunters' Halls for my daughter Motoral to bring up some of her hunting cats. And today, children, we'll have a rat and bug hunt!'

Everybody at the long tables cheered. A hunt was more fun than lessons, or work!

She nodded in satisfaction. 'Right. Both tides, of course, nobody can sleep through this! Oldest kilts and boots, and heavy gloves, and all the pets. Right, off you go and get ready!'

Soon all the children and the younger adults of the House were back among the painted pillars of the big central Hall, chattering and excited, waving shark-rib bug-swatters. Many carried rats in their arms, or held cats on leashes. Cats were undependable; when they got excited they could go for a pet rat as quickly as a wild one, and it was best not to take chances.

Motoral walked in, a big, solid woman, the leashes of four of her hunting cats firm in her strong hands. They posed elegantly beside her, tall as her waist, growling gently, spotted red and black on silver, and their slitted golden eyes froze the rats and the smaller cats in awe and fear.

Normally, Motoral would have gone over to Chooker to chat. Today, though, she just glared fiercely at her little sister. Chooker wasn't wearing the First Daughter pendant, not for something as rough as a bug hunt, but she felt Motor's resentment. She moved closer to Mungith for support, holding Peepik firm in spite of his eager wriggles. He wasn't a big fighting rat, not much bigger than Chooker's foot, but he was older than she was, knew what was happening, and was chittering with excitement.

Mungith had a young golden rat, Meelin. Though she was twice as big as Peepik, and he had been training her for a sixty-tide, this was her first real hunt. They both twitched nervously.

Mother called for silence. 'We'll do the same as usual— chase them inwards, to the back store-rooms or up into the ceiling ventilation holes to the roof.'

'And we'll be waiting there!' The oldsters, who couldn't go rummaging round the stuffy back tunnels, cheered.

'Now be careful! Wild rats are dangerous, especially giant ones. Their bites are poisonous, and they'll attack you if you get too close,' Distom warned them. 'We'll wait in the Hall. If you see the big one, yell for help. Don't tackle it alone!'

In the outside rooms, the Office and Mother's and Father's rooms and the Kitchen, all the furniture was gently moved into the centre and the rugs lifted. Then the people with cats spread out, poking into every crack in the mosaic floors and painted walls. The cats sniffed and clawed where they could hear bugs behind loose plasterwork, to show their owners where to bang and break through.

Flickers of movement started where big flat insects scurried incredibly fast, looking for dark corners. The cats jumped wildly as cockroaches scuttled between their paws.

Chooker dropped her pet. 'Go, Peepik!' she screeched— and cheered as he beat Mungith's rat to the first cockroach.

'One! Bet you Peepik gets more than your Meelin! A tooth for each extra?'

'Match!' Mung yelled in agreement, and cheered as Meelin chased and caught one. 'Yay! Good girl! Flush 'em out, flush 'em out!'

More bugs suddenly poured up from the gratings in the corners, away from the smallest youngsters and their cats wriggling beneath the raised floors of the rooms. The rats pounced. 'Eh, don't eat them, silly dodo!' Mungith scolded.

'Train her better!' Chooker screeched gleefully as Peepik dropped his third and instantly dived for the next. 'That's how it's done! We'll get two to your one! Go on, Peepik! Yay!'

When they judged it was clear, they sealed off the air vents in the floor and ceiling with hardset gel, and moved in to the Hall, the next row in, to do it all over again. And again, and again, panting and cheering and sweating as they worked deeper into the rock, past the dormitories, into the back store-rooms. Everyone was scraped and scratched and covered in dirt and dust from bundles and sacks that hadn't been moved in sixty-tides. Mother was fuming at the amount of damage she found in the stores.

Meelin was rapidly learning what was expected, and her score passed Peepik's. 'Twenty-three? Huh! Meelin's got twenty-six! What was that about training, eh?' Mungith jeered.

As they moved deeper, they caught the occasional flicker of a tail, or glimpse of black fur or white teeth. Each time, they yelled for Motoral, but she just waited. 'We'll get it at the back,' she grunted to any question.

At last, in the furthest storeroom, as usual, the last bugs and the rats were trapped. All the children crowded towards the door to watch the fight, but Motoral sharply ordered them to stand clear. 'Let me see!' she ordered.

She lifted the edge of the curtain, and peered in. Her face tightened.

'One giant rat? There's three,' she said. 'And one's big as a riding rat, almost. Real baby-killer.'

Behind her, Mother looked shocked. 'We had no idea! Can your cats manage, Motor, or will we send for more?'

'More?' Motor's temper, already irritated, flared up. 'We don't need help! Hold the curtain down tight!' She drew her long hunting knife, took a deep breath and stepped into the room, releasing her cats as she went through the doorway.

In the corridor, two adults held down the bottom hem of the curtain. Inside the room, cat yowls and terrifying rat screeches echoed. Excitedly, the crowd in the corridor listened to the yells. 'Get him, Lallee! Eh, would you? Got you!' The curtain shook as bodies thudded into it.

Suddenly, it jerked hard, and broke free. A huge rat charged out under the loose corner, a cat screaming after it. The adults in the front of the crowd leapt aside.

Against the wall behind them, Chooker found herself in the middle of a battle.

The biggest wild rat she had ever set eyes on, high as her thighs, was using her legs as a barrier to prevent the cat from getting at it from behind. She was trapped into a corner, the huge rat crouched shrieking between her knees and biting viciously at her if she moved, and the wailing cat slashing at it with razor claws.

She hit the rat, but her light stick wasn't strong enough to give an effective blow. Over the fighting animals, her terrified eyes met Mungith's.

Like the rest he had been startled by the suddenness of the animals' appearance, but now, automatically, he answered Chooker's need. He struck at the rat with the handle of his bug-swatter. Alarmed by the movement behind it, the cat swiped backwards at his legs. He yelled at the pain, but struck again. This time his club hit the rat, which leapt at him—and the cat caught it in mid-air. Biting and struggling, they rolled across the passage on to his feet, teeth and claws ripping across his shins. The pain drove him on. 'Jump!' he yelled. As Chooker dived desperately forward, he grabbed her arms, heaved her right up and over the fight and jumped after her, his legs kicking comically sideways away from the fighting animals. The adults who were now surging forward to the rescue tugged him out of range while the cat finished off the monster rat.

Back in the Hall, where everyone was gulping cool drinks, the Silver cleaned their gashes and scratches. Chooker yelped and Mungith clenched his teeth to show bravery by not even wincing. The Doctor was concerned about one deep bite on Mungith's ankle. 'Nasty,' she said, frowning. 'Maybe we should postpone your Trial. If it goes bad out in the mines—'

'It'll be fine!' Mungith protested at once. He couldn't let anything stop his Adult Trial!

'Eh, maybe.' She nodded doubtfully. 'Go swimming in the main pool, the salt will help it, and put gel on. Call me tomorrow if it's still sore.' She turned to a child with a scraped elbow.

Chooker gazed up at Mungith with pure hero-worship in her eyes. 'You saved me!' she said. 'You got hurt for me! Thank you!' She couldn't think what else to say. Mungith blushed.

Watching them, Mother and Distom exchanged a slight smile before coming forward to congratulate Mungith on his quick thinking and courage. Chooker nodded eagerly, delighted and proud for him. Mungith expanded visibly at the praise. Yes, he had done well, hadn't he! And he hadn't even thought about impressing anyone.

The adults set to work to clear up. The youngsters dumped the dead bugs and rats in the bin that Rat House left with every House for waste food—rats ate anything—and then Mungith, hero of the hunt, led them in a laughing, boasting, triumphant procession down to the swimming pools to get clean again.

Chooker didn't go with either group. All Motoral's cats had been hurt, two quite badly, and Motoral was already at work with cloths, liniments and healing gel to clean and cover the savage bites. Chooker brought her hot water and watched carefully. Some time, she might have to do this. Besides, this was a way to get near her sister, to put things right with her.

'They were very brave, Motor,' she said. 'What monsters! Will your cats be all right?'

Motoral just grunted. 'Stupid cavies! Not even thirty rats— they should have done better than that! Clumsy dodos! Here . . . hold Pinta's leg still while I stitch this paw.'

Rather nervously, Chooker took hold, feeling the tremble in the wiry muscle under the downy silver and red fur. *Lie still, please! We're going to make you better!* she urged the cat silently; and it turned its head to glare. But although it winced and yipped as the needle slipped through the skin, it didn't struggle too hard, or bite.

'Good,' Motoral grunted. 'Softset, now.' The gel, bright pink as the lobster shell it was made of, dried fast to a tough, springy seal that killed germs and would keep the wound clean while it healed. 'That'll do.' Motoral sat back on her heels and stared at Chooker. 'You told him to keep still, didn't you? Uhuh. Like me. But you can do it to people too? A bit? I can't. Uhuh.' She sniffed, with a disgusted face. 'I'm leaving. I told Mother. I'm joining Cat House.'

Chooker sighed. 'Do you have to, Motor? We'll miss you.'

Motoral grinned sourly. 'Good.' She sniffed again. 'I don't blame you. But I couldn't stay with you as Mother. Not in peace. So . . . Better if I leave you alone.' She hesitated, and then nodded. 'Good luck. Yes, really.'

That was all she said, apart from a word or two of instruction about handling the cats, but Chooker was satisfied. Motor never said much.

41

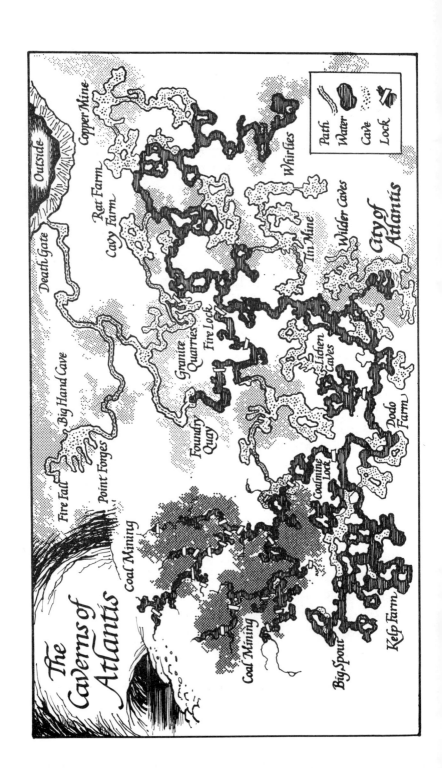

The Caverns of Atlantis

Outside
Copper Mine
Death Gate
Rat Farm
Cavy Farm
Whirlies
Fire Fall
Big Hand Cave
Point Forges
Granite Quarries
Fire Lock
Tin Mine
Wilder Caves
City of Atlantis
Foundry Quay
Lichen Caves
Coal Mining
Coalmine Lock
Dodo Farm
Coal Mining
Big Spout
Kelp Farm

Path
Water
Cave
Lock

6

After breakfast next light-tide, Mungith said Farewell to the Family. Everyone from the youngest baby in its mother's arms to old Granda Millock, Mother's grandfather, lined up to touch his hands, palms up, palms down, in the formal greeting.

Several were in tears, for they might not see him again. Some youngsters died in the Trial; some who failed killed themselves in shame, and others ran away to the Wilder Caves. They wished him luck. 'Success! Good Trial! Don't meet a Giant!'

'Go out bravely, child of Point House, and return to us an Adult!' Mother told him proudly, her mass of beaded braids quivering and glittering with her emotion.

'Good luck!' Chooker wished him, hugging him warmly. 'Come back safe!' She bit her lip so that she'd not upset him by crying.

Mungith could feel Distom projecting confidence and courage at him, and tried to smile.

Distom grinned. 'Don't worry,' he murmured, 'you'll do fine!' He took Mungith's hands and spoke loud and clear. 'May the Little Gods watch over you in your Trial, but not too closely! Fare well, Mungith. Return to Point House as Mungithak.'

As Mungith trotted down towards the harbour, he heard a shrill whistle. He glanced back. Chooker was waving from Pearl House roof. The Pearls were sticklers for Manners who would complain to Mother if they caught her there; she'd risked a public scolding for him. Her care warmed him, even more than Distom's encouragement.

A Coal was waiting for him in an empty barge by the quay,

thick with coal dust. She touched hands with him; 'Giffaral,' she said gruffly, as the Wave boatman whistled to his team of four dolphins to start hauling. Mungith looked round for a clean seat, but there wasn't one. Giffaral laughed up at him, her mouth startlingly red and white against her black skin. 'Wait till mines, lad,' she told him, not unkindly, in the Miners' oddly choked voice and clipped sentences, as if coal-dust stuffed their noses and speaking was hard. 'No shine there!'

She was short, only up to Mungith's shoulder, but solid and tough. Coal House bred small and sturdy, to fit in their tunnels, and adopted out any large children they had—often to Point, which was an off-shoot of Coal and Copper Houses. That was why Distom and Chooker were so small; Mother's grandfather had been an adopted Coal baby.

The Miners were the women of the House. Bastiyyal, who lived in the lava flows deep in the rocks, was the women's God, and caused fewer accidents for women. Besides, they said women were stronger; and it was true, their men tended to be lighter-built.

Up through a lock, they left the main Cavern complex. The barge twisted along narrow cuts and cracks, through locks and holes Mungith had never seen before. He'd thought he knew his way around the caves, but he was totally lost. At last they squeezed through a low-roofed tunnel Mungith wouldn't have even noticed into a small, fairly high cave. It was almost pitch black, for the walls' orange glow was dimmed by clinging coal-dust. Mungith climbed nervously out on to a tiny quay while the dolphins slid out of their harnesses and surged round the Wave, squealing greedily for their reward of fish.

Giffaral beckoned him up to a store-room cut in the cliffside, lit by a couple of hanging glowropes. She was quite impressed by his pack. 'Wish Father Coal fed us so well! Spare socks, uhuh. Bandages, gel, good. Blanket, for comfort, not cold where you go. Water-bottle? No?' The floppy water-sack she handed him was the whole skin of a seal.

More gear landed in his arms. 'Helmet. Boots. Pads. Gloves. Yuh, take them. Rope.' Rope? What for? Don't argue. 'Glow.' Giffaral slung a hoop of glowrope, a long sausage of dried fish-gut, glowing orange, round her neck, and gave one to Mungith. 'Keep clean, let light out. Fades, shake it. Turns green, get out fast—choking gas.' Gas? He'd never heard of this! But he mustn't let her see he was scared. 'Shovel, rake.'

'Not a pick?' Mungith asked. Giffaral only shook her head and led Mung out and up the slope, where to his surprise he found another boat, a smaller flat-bottomed barge on a narrow canal. As they clambered in, Mungith sighed. The Point chevron painted on his shoulder just after dark-dinner was smudged, and his kilt was filthy. Oh, Beliyyak! But at least it was an old one.

Two big hauling rats on a ledge at the side of the canal heaved and trotted forward, and Mungith flinched as the barge glided forward and under a low roof. 'Cheggolal, third Mother back, cut canal,' Giffaral told him. 'Pack rats before. This better.'

After a few minutes the boatwoman whistled to the rats, who slowed their steady trot to let Mungith and his guide jump off on to the path at the arched entrance to a side tunnel. The barge picked up speed again and slid off round a bend. Mungith shivered. He had never been in such darkness before, and he felt the weight of rock pressing round him as he never did in his bed at home.

Giffaral helped Mungith to slip on the reinforced leather jerkin that would save his spine scraping against the rocks above him, for the side tunnel was low, no higher than Mungith's waist. A gush of water poured from a crack high in the wall. 'Drink deep,' she told him, and filled and tied shut the big water-skin. They put on their helmets and elbow pads. 'Sling pack on chest, not on back—uhuh.' She tucked the heavy skin under one arm and the rake and the shovel under the other, jerked her head to Mungith to follow her, bent to slip under the lip of the tunnel roof—and then, to Mungith's astonishment, trotted off, head down, as fast as she could run!

He gulped and followed her. The tunnel floor was fairly smooth, but if he lifted his head to see forward, he cracked it against low rocks in the roof. If he didn't, he lost the light of his guide. He had to keep his knees bent and his back level, or his spine hit the roof. Within a hundred steps, his back, neck, knees, and thighs were aching and his head was ringing in spite of the helmet. The water was sloshing about in his stomach. He wished he'd not drunk so much. Gasping for breath, his muscles screaming, he struggled to keep up with the flickering gleam.

They passed through a couple of high natural caverns, and several old, worked-out seams—wide flat areas where the clatter of his boots echoed through ranks of supporting pillars. Mungith knew coal lay flat, like mud in a pool, sometimes two or even three arm-spans thick, not in upright walls like silver or copper.

Along the tunnels about every sixty-paces a higher, wider passing space had been dug out, where he could straighten and ease his back and his legs. But he always had to bend again, more painfully every time.

He couldn't go on! Why had he, a big-bred Point, picked a Trial where his size was a handicap? He couldn't go on!

Staggering, aching, cursing himself for stupidity, he did.

Suddenly he bumped into Giffaral. She had stopped. By the faint light of their glows, he could see her standing in an open place, grinning. 'Not bad for City boy!'

He sat down. Rather, his knees folded under him, and he collapsed on a pile of rubble. Every separate bone in his spine felt as if it had been hit with a hammer. 'What?'

Her teeth and eyes gleamed at him. 'Uhuh. Went in circle

46

to see if you'd crack in dark. Many do. No shame if you did. Good you didn't. I'll tell your Family you've begun well.'

Mungith was getting his breath back, and in spite of the aches he could feel pleased. He puffed. 'Thank you! Now what?'

'Hang up bag, pack. Stay here.' She gestured round. It was not absolutely pitch black here; the working was old enough, and far enough from the busy, dusty main tunnels, for the algae to grow again, in a dim orange glow. 'Six passages. That way, floor of level above flopped—old, abandoned. Needs filling in, stop spread. You start. Rake this rubble to far end, pile high, pack tight. Careful—don't bring more roof down. Creak or roar, press against wall, arms over face, pray to Bastiyyal. Not likely. Don't wander. Back in ten tides. Right?'

Mungith gulped. She spoke so fast, in her thick accent, he hadn't quite understood all of that—and he didn't want her to go and leave him! But he made himself nod. 'Ten tides. Right. Th-thank you.' He sat still, watching greedily as Giffaral looked at him searchingly, nodded in satisfaction, and trotted away. Her glow flickered down the tunnel, turned a corner and vanished.

He was alone. On his own for the first time ever, with no Family, no Mother or Father to call on. He almost shouted to Giffaral to come back—he suspected that she'd wait for a few minutes, just out of sight, in case he panicked and screamed for her to get him out. But no. He'd not do that. He'd begun well, she had said so; he was going to succeed!

The weight of the rock above pressed him down—don't think about it! Keep busy!

First, mark the way out—just in case. Mungith laid his pack by the entrance tunnel, where the Coal had set down the water-skin and tools. He found a level bed of sand—well, coal gravel—and knew enough to dig hollows for his shoulder and hip before he laid out his blanket as a bed. The mine was warm. Some mines, he knew, were up near the ice, but this one must be near the fire. What would happen if it erupted right into a coal mine? Don't think about that. At least, thanks to all he'd drunk, he wasn't thirsty, and wouldn't be for some time. This water had to last him for ten tides. If she came in time, and didn't forget—don't think about that, either!

Atlantans always knew where the tide was. It was low now, and he wasn't likely to sleep right through the rise and fall of a tide, so he'd be able to keep count of the tides.

He suddenly realized that he was putting off time. To pass his Trial, he had to do more than just stay here. He could do a good bit of work before he slept—he wasn't going anywhere.

He wiped dust off his glow and held it high to drive back the dark. Which tunnel was he to fill? Gingerly, for it would be a long, painful wait if he sprained or broke an ankle on the rough floor, he set out to explore. He was limping already, but if he had told the Silver his bad ankle was sore she'd have stopped his Trial. About fifty paces along, the tunnel was blocked by a long slide of rocks. Right. He had to fill it up, to stop any more roof collapses. Flop, she'd called it.

He started raking rubble towards the tunnel. To his annoyance, for he had thought he was fit, his muscles started complaining very soon that they weren't used to this kind of exercise, and he had to take a break. However, he started again as soon as he could, and developed a rhythm of work and rest, changing from rake to shovel and back, that kept him out of too much pain but shifted quite a satisfactory amount of stones.

Far too soon, he thought, Mungith was starving and exhausted, but he'd not let himself stop until he felt it was high tide again. He had made a good start. He laid down his rake, and took off his gloves. He hadn't wanted to take them in case the Coal thought he was soft, but now he was glad she had insisted. They must have saved him lots of blisters already.

Mother had packed his food for each meal in separate numbered parcels, wrapped in clingy kelp film. He opened the first; cold roast dodo, chewy pickled sea-squirts rolled in laver-weed, eight fresh puffs with his favourite spicy spread, sweet biscuits—left-overs from the Welcome Dinner for Prentastal and her man, delicious. He had enough water to clear the worst of the dust from his nose; down here, he didn't need to bother washing!

He was tempted to open the next parcel and see what was for breakfast, but no; he must have something to look forward to. Firmly, he put the unopened packets back in his pack and tucked it under his head for a pillow. Eh, he was aching all over, but it would ease off.

Something was missing. It swept over him, now he had nothing to occupy his mind. He was fed, warm, reasonably comfortable—but he was alone. For the first time in his life, there was no other person within sound of him. No breathing, no coughing or sniffing, no rustle of movement from his cousins in the other cubicles of the Nursery. No warm, comforting purr of thoughts all round him, just below awareness. Nothing. An aching silence, coldness, emptiness of mind, everywhere . . .

His heart was jumping in fright at the little ticks and creaks and groans, the voice of the rock moving imperceptibly, that you never noticed out in the huge City cavern. But he'd manage. Only another nine tides. He rubbed his arms to get rid of the dodo-flesh and loosen his tight muscles. He'd manage. If this was what it took to be an Adult, he could do it.

While he slept, the Coal crept up the passage till she could hear his even breathing. Yes, he was doing well. She'd check every couple of tides, to help if he broke down completely. But it was important he didn't know about it, that he thought he was on his own.

Next tide, Mungith woke with a start. Why was it so dark?

And so silent? His back hurt . . . his bed was flat and hard . . . oh, of course!

Something scuttled in the darkness. Rats? Cockroaches? Giants—don't be silly!

Move—yes, move! Oh, his arms and shoulders! His fingers felt swollen, and he worked them for a while, to ease them. And his back, and knees—and his ankle! He could scarcely move his foot. He groped for the glow. Eh, Beliyyak! The whole joint was very puffy and red.

Moving slowly for the stiffness he got out the roll of bandages and the jar of ointment for scrapes, although he didn't think it would be much use. But he had some soft-gel in his pack. He could put it on as a poultice. He should have listened to the Doctor—but he'd been too keen to get on with his Trial. Silly. Childish? Yes. Well, he'd just have to get on with it now. That was what Adults did.

Now what? Have a drink, see what Mother had given him for breakfast—and then get busy again. His pack had been nibbled, even right under his head, and the water skin—if that had been punctured, he'd really have been in trouble. He found a broken shark-rib pick handle, cut two pegs from it and jammed them in the roof, and managed to sling his supplies between them. That was what the rope was for. He should have done it before sleeping, as the Coal had said.

Suddenly, right above his head, the rock creaked loudly. A stone fell.

He found himself far down the exit tunnel, flat on his face where he had tripped and fallen. Half stunned, unable to breathe for terror, he lay flat. Osiriyyak, Great God of Rock, turn your eye from me!

Nothing happened.

How did the Coals do this, all tide, every tide? And the Golds and Granites, the other mining Families? He had always felt superior to them, their snuffly breathing through open mouths, their smallness, their red-rimmed eyes. But they were braver than him, far, far braver!

He finally made himself get up, turn and go back to the cave. If the roof came down, well, he might be under it—or he might not. Only two years before, eighteen Coals had been trapped by an explosion. The Queen had almost decided she must give herself to the whirlpools as a sacrifice to calm the Little Gods' anger, when the Miners had unexpectedly been found all alive. 'Beliyyak, watch over me,' Mungith prayed aloud, and didn't add the usual 'but not too closely.' The closer Beliyyak kept an eye on him, for the moment, the happier he'd be!

For eight more tides Mungith worked away, filling the collapsed passage bit by bit. He had never realized how difficult it was to use a shovel while you were kneeling under a low roof, but he was quite pleased with himself. The Coals could probably—well, certainly—do it better and faster, but he wasn't doing too badly for a non-Miner.

Twice, he cried himself to sleep. But he'd never tell anyone that. Not even Chooker. Especially not Chooker.

To pass the time, and hide from the aching silence and solitude, he practised his drumming. Mica House organized a band of musicians from all the Houses that played for every important occasion in the City. Mungith planned to audition for drummer with them. He whittled drumsticks out of the old pick-handle, and rattled rolls, riffs, and tattoos on any convenient rock—there was no shortage—singing away merrily, imagining the full band playing with him.

Then one tide, just after his dinner, it dawned on him that he had an echo.

Nobody ever noticed the normal background resonance from the cave roof and walls. This was different; a half-hearted, almost nervous echo, that started a few seconds after he stopped, tried to copy what he'd just drummed, and usually didn't finish it.

Mungith sat, drumsticks loose in his hands, his mouth open in astonishment. Then he tried a simple, slow, four-beat pattern. It was copied. Then another; and it was copied, too. A more complicated one—no, the 'echo' broke down half-way through.

Then it tapped first. One tap, then two, then three. And waited.

What was it? Bastiyyal, coming up from the fire flows to destroy him? Scarcely—a Goddess would be able to play any riff a human could.

Could it be a Giant? Mungith shivered. But no, that was only a story to thrill children. Nobody had ever seen one, not for sure.

Nobody that had come back to tell about it.

Eh, rubbish! It was more likely a hurt Miner, trapped by a roof fall somewhere, trying to find a way out through the old collapsed workings. Or a strayed Coal child, lost while playing hide-and-seek, or going into the mine as a dare.

Of course it was.

He tapped, copying the one-two-three pattern. It came back again, faster, as if pleased to have made contact. It was probably a lost child.

Where had the noise come from? The next tunnel along? He stood up, wincing on his bad ankle, and stooped a dozen paces into the other tunnel before trying again. Yes, the reply sounded clearer. Further along—try again—yes, he was heading the right way. But it seemed to be above him. As he moved forward, he found himself in one of the passing spaces, where the roof rose higher. He tapped again; this time, the reply seemed to come from directly overhead. And he could hear footsteps, now—

A creak, a crunching growl, a roar. A brief dazzle of light. He tried to leap for the wall, as the Coal had told him to do, but his bad ankle gave way.

The roof fell in.

7

Slowly, slowly, Mungith realized he wasn't dead. He had no idea how long he'd been there, petrified by terror, his ears filled with din and his eyes and mouth with dust, while chunks of rock thudded on his shoulders and head, and bounced and rolled against his legs.

The dust in the air was settling, he could breathe, just. He choked, coughed, and spat, and gradually got rid of most of the dust in his throat. His head was spinning, he felt sick. Agony burned in his right forearm. He was cut and bruised all over, and he must have been unconscious for...a minute, an hour, a tide? Cuts and bruises were nothing. He'd survive.

It was pitch black. All the walls' glow was smothered in dust, and his little light must be under the stones somewhere. Beliyyak had watched over him, or he'd be dead now. But not too closely, or the rock wouldn't have fallen. Oh, well. Gods did as they pleased. He was grateful for even so much help.

He couldn't move his feet. Or his left arm. Not a fraction. His right? Yes. It hurt, oh, how it hurt! But he could move it. Maybe he'd had the arm up over his head to protect himself. With care, he felt round. He was sitting in stones as if in water, settled tight and sharp round him half-way up his chest. He couldn't breathe deeply, couldn't move his feet at all. Couldn't move couldn't move—

With a surge of relief, he thought of Distom, back in the House. Distom, worrying about him, trying to sense him, sensitive to all his Family but turning his mind specially towards Mungith, the one on Trial, in danger, the one who might need him now. Mentally and aloud, Mungith shouted for help. 'Distomak! Distom! Please, help! If you didn't hear me while the rock was falling, please hear me now! Please! Come now! Now! Right away!'

Distom would hear him, and send help. He must!

Of course he would. Mungith gritted his teeth—not difficult, with all this dust in his mouth. The silly joke, flicking through his mind, calmed him more than anything. If he could joke, he wasn't too badly off.

But he couldn't stay here. He was on Trial. He had to do everything he could, not give in, get out if he could before the rescuers arrived. If they did . . .

Don't doubt it. They'd come.

In spite of the fierce pain, he started to push the stones away from his trapped left arm with his bruised right hand. After a while he could wriggle and heave it free. This arm, stiff and bruised but less damaged, could move faster. Slowly, he cleared round his chest. He found his glow under the stones, but it had been ripped open and the glowing paste inside was leaking. It would soon be smothered in coal dust. Eh, better than nothing! He smeared the leaking stuff over his chest.

The broken stones were sharp-edged, painful to shift, and some were fairly large and heavy. Most were small, fist-sized chunks and gravel; nothing crushing, thank Beliyyak! He worked on, sobbing gently as he heaved them up and away to clatter into the blackness.

Something moaned.

Mungith jumped, startled, and then remembered. Eh, yes, the lost person. Whoever it was must have been walking in the old workings above, and been too heavy for the cracked roof. 'Hey! Are you badly hurt?' he called.

After a few seconds, another moan answered him. A man's voice.

'Don't worry. I'm getting free. I'll be with you in a few minutes!' Mungith called. He worked harder, and kept talking, to reassure the man. He must be hurt badly, or he'd

54

have answered. 'I've cleared most of the stones off my legs. Not long now. Ow . . . that one's heavy . . . got it. Eh, I've got one foot out!' One or two toes hurt so much they could be broken. At least the pain of his bad ankle was gone, lost in the greater pains of the rock fall. 'That's that big one . . . I can move my foot . . . just get this rock a bit more over . . . another nail gone . . . got a grip now . . . and up . . . got it! I'm out!'

He heaved his feet out of the hole and lay back for a rest, gasping, nursing his bleeding fingers. But he must see if the other person was trapped too. He tucked his hurt arm inside his leather jerkin and rolled laboriously on to his knees. Ouch! One of his knee pads had come off, and one of his boots. He must dig for the boot. He'd need it to get out, and if he lost the hole he might never find it again.

Wincing, he felt about in the hollow left by his legs. Almost the first thing he touched was the knee pad. That encouraged him to feel round deeper and further in spite of the hurt to his torn fingers. Thanks to Beliyyak, here was the boot! He gripped the soft hide and tugged.

It tore off.

Hot tears started to flow, but he sniffed hard to drive them back. He'd not give in! He groped among the stones and gravel till he felt leather again, grasped it, twisted and jiggled, until at last the boot came out. He sat for a long time, clutching it, grinning foolishly in triumph and relief, before another moan from the darkness woke him up. Get a move on, Mungith! Or you'll never be Mungithak!

He emptied the boot and put it on. The laces had broken, but even one-handed he managed to tie the ends together somehow. The knee pad had lost a buckle, but he still had his knife, in its sheath at his waist; he cut a strip off his jerkin to tie it on with. The relief was enormous; he could move across the stones in—well, almost in comfort! In his legs, at least.

'Hey! Where are you? I'm coming!' he called. Another moan answered him. He crawled towards the sound, feeling ahead of him, peering over the fading light from the glow paste, trying not to yelp when his fingers and shins landed on jagged rock.

He touched something soft. It whimpered and winced away. 'It's all right, it's just me,' Mungith said reassuringly. Here was a leg—a knee, yes, wrapped in a kind of tube of cloth. Far too big for a child. The foot would be this way—

His fingers found a hand, not a foot. This was an arm. Huge. Enormous.

A Giant? No nonono . . .

He jumped back, and knocked a rock aside with his knee. A dazzling light flashed out from under it, to fill the broken cave with brilliance.

It was a Giant, lying there, half hidden under fallen rocks. Its head wasn't much bigger than his own, but its hand was twice the size of his.

The huge hand twitched, turned and grasped his wrist.

It was too much. He fainted.

From the minute Mungith left the House, Chooker roamed restlessly, unable to settle to anything. Her friends tried to reassure her, but she only snarled at them till they snapped back, 'Just because your boy's away, you needn't peck like a dodo cock!'

She started staying up during dark-tide to be near Distom. When Mother objected to the child changing tides, Distom gently suggested that it would do his young sister no harm to learn about a Father's work in a House. She wasn't sharing a cubicle now, so she had no sleeping partner to disturb. Besides, it was only for a few tides. So Chooker dumped cushions in a corner behind the big slate desk in the Office, sat there cuddling Peepik, and watched, listened, and learned as long as she could stay awake; and the emptiness because Mungith was gone, the shadowy lost feeling, faded in Distom's kindly warmth.

Distomak was in charge of the trade of the House. He didn't run the big smithy and workshops by which Family members earned a living, but he bought the raw materials and household supplies, and sold the finished products, spearheads or anchors, sequins or knives.

When he first became Point Father, some people thought that such a weakling would be easy to beat or cheat. However, after the first would-be trickster left in tears and spent the next tides anxiously repaying previous victims, he was seldom bothered in that way.

Naturally, Distom did not use his power to gain an unfair advantage. He couldn't. If any Senser, especially a Father, tried to do so, the other Sensers combined against him. Atlantis was more important than any one person. In any case, as he said, if people left feeling resentful or aggrieved about their dealings with him, he felt their emotions and suffered.

During the ninth tide Mungith was away, when Chooker was eagerly looking forward to his return, Loop Father was trying to sell Distom a new medicine. 'It's made from sea-scorpion venom—with some additions! Wonderful pain-stopper. Burn off your hand, you'll feel absolutely nothing. Not a twinge. Costly, of course, but worth every tooth. Specially good for Point—burns, accidents at the forge and so on—but even the Spirals can have illness, roof collapse—'

Distom shot to his feet, clutching his desk. In her corner, Chooker awoke, shrieking, 'Mung! Mung!'

After a moment's shock the Loop yelled, 'Help! Point Father's in trouble!'

Already the rings of the door curtain were clattering aside. Point Mother, charging from her bedroom next door, pushed through the helpers and took in the scene in one fast stare. 'Narleen, my smelling salts, fast. Distom, is it Mungith? Come on, my dear, we can't help till we know what's happened. Stop screaming, Chooker! Stop at once! The rest of you, calm down!'

Narleen ran in with the bottle of guano salts. Mother held it under Distom's nose. He coughed and choked, and clawed at Mother's hands, shoving the bottle away. 'What is it, Distom? Is it Mungith?'

Controlling himself, Distom nodded. 'A fall. He's not dead, I can still feel him, but hurt.' His eyes stared out beyond the walls of the room. 'We must help him!'

'Of course.' Mother was nodding. 'Frentock, run to Coal House, we need someone who knows the mine where Mungith is, who can understand what Distom senses better than we can. Narleen, run down to the harbour, hire us the fastest boat. Trooshill, go to Silver House for a Doctor to be ready to leave with the boat. Hush, Chook. Quiet, now—and everyone else, quiet. Now, Distom, relax. Think about nothing, let your mind empty. No worry, no urgency—we'll see to everything. Just open your mind, think of Mung. Mungith. What's he doing?'

'I don't know. I've lost contact.' Distom nodded to Mother. 'I need a mindreach.'

She looked doubtful. 'They're dangerous—'

'It could save Mungith's life!' The little man was stern. The pills exhausted him for days. But when it was necessary... Mother nodded reluctantly, and took a soft capsule from the red jar.

Lying back, Distom stared at the roof. Urgently, helped by the drug, he felt out to Mungith. 'He's trapped, hurt—but not badly. It's all dark.' By the time a delicate young Coal man panted in, they were all relaxing at the news that Mung was recovering, digging himself out.

'Be searching already, Point Mother,' the Coal reassured them. Although he'd never been up a mine in his life, he still followed the short Coal pattern of speech. 'Sound of fall travels fast, far, start rescue at once.'

58

'Wait . . . wait.' Distom flapped a hand for silence. 'There's someone else there. I can't quite—it's male. Lost. A boy, maybe, who wanted to be a Miner like his sisters? And ran away there, to prove he could do it?'

'Can't be!' The Coal shook his head doubtfully. 'None missing.' He made a face. 'Go myself, tell them. Find out.' He didn't look happy about it.

'Mungith's not exactly where he was.' Distom was shaken but calm. 'He had to go to search for the other person. Not far, I think, but . . . I'll go with you.'

'You can't,' Mother protested. Distom opened his mouth. She glared at him. 'No!'

'We'll find him.' The Coal turned to leave and found a girl, not much taller than himself, clasping his arm.

'Take me.' Chooker was scared, but somebody had to go. 'I can sense Mung.'

'Got own Sensers, girl. No,' the Coal said flatly.

'They're not his Family. I can find him quickly.' Chooker looked at Mother for help. 'I can always find him, Mother, can't I? And if he's hurt, or the other person is, even a few minutes could make the difference between living and dying. Please!'

The Coal shook his head again. 'You're untrained, scared.'

'Just take her,' Mother said. 'Even if she's afraid to go into the tunnels when you get there, you mustn't waste time arguing here.'

'Uhuh.' Unconvinced, but hurrying, the Coal turned to the door.

Distom gasped. Chooker, hugging Mother hard in thanks, stiffened and yelped.

'What is it?' Mother demanded.

Distom rubbed his forehead with both hands, his face twisted with pain. 'Terror—I couldn't get it, Mung has fainted. Hurry!' The little man gestured urgently. 'Run. Run!'

At the door, Loop Father pressed his jar of pills into

Chooker's hand. 'Take these. They kill pain, they may help. Bastiyyal aid you!'

'Thanks,' Chooker called absently, already half-way down the passage.

The Waves ran a couple of small, fast canoes, with six dolphins, to carry urgent messages. One had been already moved out to the end of the pier to save time when Chooker, the Coal, and a young Silver swarmed down the slippery steps, and the dolphins were heaving the light shell into the current even before Chooker sat down. Scarcely noticing the jolt, she only urged them, 'Hurry, please hurry!'

8

Driven by the emergency, they travelled at racing speed, lifted the canoe up the locks while the dolphins dived through the sluice gates, and were bumping the mine quay in a tenth of the time Mungith's heavy barge had taken. A Miner ran down from the store-room to the quay, looking worried. 'Big flop. Can't find boy.' She shook her head. 'Bad.'

Chooker nodded. She'd known she'd be needed! She stared round, shivering and stifled already in the darkness, the heaviness of the air. She could never do her Trial here! But she must go on, right into the low tunnels. Mung needed her.

As the newcomers were fitted out with glows and helmets, spine-guards and boots, the Silver and even the Coal seemed as nervous as Chooker. Oddly, that calmed her nerves. If Adults were afraid, it was no shame to her. And if they could do it, she could.

On the canal, the barge driver urged her rats to a gallop along to the side tunnel. 'Good luck!' she called, waving while Chook forced herself to bend and go into the smothering blackness. The cheerful voice heartened her as she tried not to sob in terror, to concentrate on Mung. He needed her! Nothing else mattered, not her fear, her trouble in breathing; nothing!

They were led straight. Before Chook's legs and back were unbearably sore, they arrived at the nearest passing place to the face of the fall. Giffaral greeted them grimly. 'Four tunnels down. Rotten above. Got to dig through, if boy's . . .' she paused.

'He's still alive!' Chooker panted.

'You feel him? Good!' Giffaral grinned, teeth flashing. 'Senser can't feel him clearly. Not Coal.' She nodded towards an old man sitting at one side, staring with a wide, blank gaze.

It was a shock to the Coal, too, to hear about the stranger in the mine. She turned to the Senser. 'Cawriss, anyone else there? How many there? How many, Cawriss?'

The old man gazed placidly at them. Chooker was sure he'd never been capable of a Trial to become Adult. He was a dull, an eternal child, cared for all his life because of his special talent. Now he sighed deeply. 'Two,' he said, and giggled unexpectedly. 'Two. Big and small. Two. Left and right. Two. Up and down. Light and—'

'Uhuh, stop!' Giffaral told him firmly. 'Where? Where are they, Cawriss?'

The man sighed again, turned and pointed vaguely at the rock. 'There. There. There. There.' Each time, his finger moved to a slightly different direction.

'See?' Giffaral said. 'You do better?'

Chooker had been trying to feel for Mungith ever since they had stopped moving. Now she pointed fairly confidently, slightly left of where the Coal Senser had directed them. 'That way. But—I don't know—higher up, I think.'

Giffaral considered. 'Uhuh. How far?'

That was harder. 'Er . . . straight to him . . . about . . . about four sixty-paces. Or a little more.'

'Uhuh.' The Coal jerked her head, beckoning. She led Chooker back the way they had come and then up a steep passage, the other Miners trotting behind. They branched left, right, crossed an open space, stopped. 'Where now?'

Chooker thought. 'Down . . . that way. Not as far.'

She was led along further, to try again; and again. Her head ached with concentrating, fighting the stuffiness, the fearsome pressure of the rock all round, the suffocation . . .

At last, Giffaral nodded. 'Placed him.' With a rock, she banged at the foot of the wall; tap, ti-ti-tap tap; and waited. After a moment, the reply came, to finish the pattern; ti-ti tap. 'Yuh!' she shouted. 'Awake, too! Not where we thought. Easy to reach. You saved work, time—good. Out in half a tide, nugget!'

We're coming, Mung! We're coming! Chooker thought as hard as she could. Would he hear her? She had never tried to send before . . . Yes, his fear lightened. He knew she was near. But beyond his fear she could sense a strange mixture of astonishment and glee.

With picks and drills the Miners attacked the side of the tunnel. They broke through into workings behind, found a wall of debris, and began to make a triangular burrow into it. Chooker followed them, passing in roof props, saying how much further they had to go, handing round a water-skin, helping to rake back the rubble from their digging to leave a clear passage, until they started working more cautiously in case they came across a soft body among the stones.

Then, at last, one Miner gave a shout of triumph. Her spade had pushed through the rocks. A brilliance like a lava flow shone through from the space beyond. And Mung's voice shouted in reply!

We've found him! Chooker shouted with her mind to Distom, back at home. He'd hear her, with the drug's help, and tell the Family.

Mungith called, 'What kept you? Come on in, I've got a surprise for you!'

Giffaral snorted approval. She nodded to her mates to dig into the rubble again.

Chooker could feel Mung's relief—and triumph, now that he felt safe. He'd found something marvellous. Was it this light? No, it was more than that . . .

Giffaral wriggled through the gap they had made—and yelled in astonishment and fright. They heard Mungith laugh. 'Don't worry—it won't hurt you!'

The woman turned to clearing a bigger entry hole, and her

teeth gleamed as she grinned through at them. 'Hurry see!' she called.

As each Miner clambered through the hole, she gasped, exclaimed. Chooker was almost bursting with curiosity. She crawled across the jagged stones, up through the hole into the dazzle, and stood up. Then, in her turn, she gaped in shock.

Lying half buried in rocks was a Giant. A real Giant. Its arm was as big as Mung's leg. It wasn't dead, for it was breathing, but it was unconscious. It must have been caught in the same rock-fall that had hurt Mung—thank Bastiyyal, or it could have killed him! 'Are you all right, Mung?' she demanded.

'Fine!' he nodded. 'Thanks for coming, Chooker, but I'm fine.'

She sniffed, as much to hold back tears of relief at his survival as to show her contempt for his denial of the help she had given. Of course he'd needed her—and of course he wouldn't admit it, especially not in front of Coals. Boys!

The Coals were clambering round the monster, studying it. 'It's a Giant,' Mungith said smugly. He'd had a good deal of time to get used to the idea. He held up the rod that made the light. 'This belongs to it. Look—if you put your hand over it, you can see all the bones, it's so bright. But it's not lava-hot, just warm.'

'Kill it,' a Miner whispered. 'Now, before wakes.' She hefted her pick.

'No,' Mungith declared firmly. 'It was awake earlier. It didn't hurt me—and it could have, I'd—I was unconscious. Right beside it. It's hurt—it has a broken arm, I think, and ribs, and maybe legs as well under the rock there. It fell through the roof.'

'Uhuh.' The Coal leader nodded. 'You hurt?'

'A few bumps, Giffaral. And I think my arm's broken.' Mungith was casually heroic.

Reluctantly remembering why he was here, the Silver turned from studying the Giant to check Mungith. As his forearm was splinted and a couple of toes were pulled straight, Mungith winced and grunted, but he managed not to scream. He got his reward; Chooker smiled at him. Wasn't her big cousin brave!

When she looked back at the Giant she jumped and exclaimed. Its eyes were open.

It spoke. They couldn't understand a word. Then, to their astonishment, it started crying. Tears trickled from its eyes, leaving white tracks in the coal dust.

The Coals were wary, but Mungith bent down to touch it, to soothe it.

The City Coal dragged him back. 'Don't!' he ordered him angrily. 'Could be trick!'

'It's hurt—and it didn't hurt me before,' Mungith protested. The Silver nodded approval.

'Don't care—dangerous!' the Coal insisted.

Mungith tutted, and then had an idea. 'Let Chooker see if she can read its mind. She's a Senser, a bit at least. She can tell us if it's safe to touch it.'

'Me?' Chooker was appalled. 'Touch a Giant? You're daft as a dodo! Or you think I am!'

'Yes, go on,' Mungith urged her. He didn't want his great discovery to be killed, not down here in the mine before everybody had seen it! 'We'll be ready to save you if it attacks.'

'How kind!' Chooker exclaimed. 'What if it moves too fast?' But the Coals were nodding slowly. And if he wanted it . . . 'Eh, I suppose I can try.'

Around Chooker everyone poised shovels and picks. Reluctantly, Chooker knelt down beside the beast. She braced herself, and smiled to reassure it, and to encourage herself. Gingerly, she patted its hand and took it in hers. It lay tense in her clasp. What huge coarse fingers! At last, the hand relaxed slightly—and suddenly her mind brushed the Giant's.

It was ready to fight, terrified, here in the dark, surrounded by—she saw herself through its mind—fearsome little black people. The black was coal dust, of course. It was used to light.

She stiffened her mind against the jagged strangeness of its mind, and concentrated on radiating reassurance. *Don't worry, calm, we won't hurt you,* she told it until at last its fear faded. She sat back on her heels, wiping sweat from her forehead. It was far harder to send than to read. 'No, it's not dangerous,' she said. 'Not now, at least. It's afraid, and hurt, and lost.'

'Right!' Mungith exclaimed in satisfaction. 'We can take it home.'

The Coal man exclaimed in horror. 'Huh? Giant in City?'

'Why not?' Mungith demanded. 'It can't hurt anybody.'

'Not now, but when it's recovered? Could kill us all!'

'We'd watch to see it didn't. It could work in our forges. We can't just kill it!' Kill his find? Not if he could help it!

'No, indeed,' the Silver agreed. He was washing the Giant's arm, muttering to himself in amazement. 'Look at that, now,' he said, fussy as Silvers tended to be. 'It saw me dealing with Mungith, and it's not resisting me. It's even turning its arm to help me. It seems to have intelligence. Ah, there we are. I thought so—the artery's cut.' The Giant gasped as a dust-clot came away and blood spurted from a deep cut.

The Silver tutted gently, lifted a hand and concentrated. The Giant gasped again as the flow stopped. 'Never seen a Doctor stop blood before? Don't worry, we'll mend it!' The Silver smiled at his huge patient, wiped away the blood and started spreading on a patch of softset. 'Eh, of course we can't kill it! Not unless we have to, if it turns out to be untameable. And I don't think it will, somehow.'

'Uhuh. Can't,' Giffaral agreed. She grinned at her Coal cousin's annoyance. 'But work in mines.'

'It's mine! Well, Point's! I found it!' Mungith exclaimed.

'We'll rescue it!' she retorted.

'And rescue you!' the City Coal added.

They all glared at each other.

Chooker puffed in exasperation at the waste of time. She didn't want the Giant in Atlantis, but if Mungith did, she'd support him.

There was one way in which any Adult could end any argument. Could a child do it? She realized suddenly that she wasn't just any Roof brat! She had rank of her own. 'I am Point First Daughter. I call on the King and Queen to judge this matter.'

An appeal to the King and Queen had to go to them at once, with no further discussion. Rather relieved, Mungith and the Coals nodded to Chooker and turned to digging out the Giant.

When the monster was moved it cried out in pain. Chooker remembered her gift of pain-stops from the Loops. The Silver, slapping softset on cuts and grazes, nodded. 'Oh, yes, dear, certainly, they're very good. Give one to Mungith.'

'What about the Giant?' she asked.

The Silver considered. 'It's so much bigger—but they might be a poison for Giants. Um. Try two. That should be safe enough, on a brute that size.'

Mungith took his quickly, and whistled. 'I feel better already. They work really fast!' Chooker didn't know if the monster would know what to do with them, but after a doubtful look at them it heaved its shoulders in a deep sigh and swallowed the pills without fuss. After only a few moments, it sighed again, with release. She felt the tenseness of its pain and fear fade away, replaced to her astonishment by an excited curiosity.

While the Silver strapped up the hurt arm, which was badly cut and bruised but not broken, and the Coals worked to dig out the monster, Mungith was shining the light all round the cavern. It came from one end of a chunky rod of hardened black kelp stem, reflected, they could see, by a tiny concave mirror. 'Good idea, eh?' the Coal man said. 'Tell Left Triangle House—they make mirrors. But how make little light, eh? No room for candle.'

The Giant was watching them. It beckoned with its free hand, reaching for the light. Mungith was tempted to hold on to it—after all, he had found it—but he grimaced and handed it back. The Giant nodded. 'Tawch,' it said. 'Tawch.' It pointed a vast finger at a lump on the side of the rod, and pressed. The light stopped, with a click, and started again with another.

It nodded to Mungith. 'Tawch,' it repeated. It reached out, took Mungith's good hand very gently, and pressed one of his fingers on the bump. It went in, and clicked. The light stopped. 'Tawch,' it said in the darkness, and pressed. With a click, the light started again.

'That's what makes it stop and start, that bump on the tawch thing!' Mungith exclaimed. He pressed it twice; the light blinked out and in. 'Yay!' He grinned down at the Giant. 'Tawch!' he said, and stopped and started the light. 'Tawch! Look, I can speak to it!'

The Giant was grinning and nodding—straight forward, not to the side like proper people, but they could see that it was agreeing. It held out the tawch to Mungith, with a kind of formal gesture. 'Tawch foryoo,' it said firmly, and gave it to the young man.

'Present!' the Coal leader grunted, rather resentfully.

Preening himself, Mungith flashed the tawch all over, off and on, till they complained about the effect on their eyes. 'Oh, all right!' he said rather pettishly. He wanted to play with it!

Chooker nudged him. She had noticed the Coal's annoyance. 'It would be a nice thank you gift,' she whispered to him.

Mungith sniffed. But yes, it would. He did owe the Coals a

lot—it wasn't their fault the roof had fallen in on him! 'I suppose so,' he whispered back.

Formally, fingers on his chest, he bowed to the Coal leader. 'Giffaral of Coal House, this tawch will be of more use in the darkness of the mines than in the bright light of Point forges,' he announced. 'Please accept it as a gift from Point House, in gratitude for your care and labour.'

Giffaral beamed as she accepted it. 'Good boy!' she grunted. 'Good Manners.' Mungith winked to Chooker. That was a good idea he'd had!

The Giant was rapidly dug out. Its shinbone was broken; with the strength of the Miners to pull it straight, the Silver soon had it in place and splinted with a few strips of shark-rib in hardset gel. He plastered its other cuts and bruises. 'It'll have to wait till the City for more. I can sense where there's damage, and control bleeding, of course, and I'm a bone-setter, just what you want in an accident. But there are far better than me at healing. Eh, yes. They'll soon mend it!'

The Giant was lifted carefully on to a stretcher and carried to the canal at a trot—Coals were experts at handling heavy weights in tight spaces. The tawch was useful; they could see much further in the dusty tunnels, and move faster. Even in its weakness and hurt, the Giant stared round in awe at the mine, the hauling rats, the canal, the boats, the colourful caverns as it was carried along.

Distom had passed on word of their safety as soon as he had sensed it from Chooker. Every boat in the harbour was out to greet them. All the Coals and Points, and half the rest of the City, it seemed, were on the quay, crowding round the white gowns of the King and Queen, cheering and clapping and stamping, whistling and waving as the big coal barge drew up beside the quay and they saw the immense bundle that was the Giant.

Making the most of the event, Giffaral climbed the quay steps and bowed to Coal Mother and Father, and to the King

69

and Queen. 'Chooker, of Point House. Brave girl,' she called into the eager silence. 'Dared mine. Helped save cousin.' She beckoned, and everyone cheered as Chooker ran up the steps to Point Mother's hug.

The Coal raised her hand for silence again. 'Great find,' she called. 'Giant! And great wonder!' She held up the tawch and pressed the bulge. At the beam of light, gushing right across the cavern to light up the far wall, there was a gasp; and then deafening applause.

Giffaral beckoned Mungith to come up the steps.

Normally Mungith would have hated being seen in such a mess, but now he was proud of it. His filth, torn kilt, bruises, sling, and bandages showed how dangerous his Trial had been. Hoping everyone noted how bravely he bore his wounds, he limped up the steps to bow stiffly to the King and Queen. 'My duty to Atlantis and my House,' he declared. Nobody could hear him in the din, but everyone knew the formula. 'I have finished my Trial, and I claim Adulthood.'

Beside him, Giffaral bowed also, as his examiner. 'Trial complete. Good boy. Good Trial. Good Adult, uhuh!' she grunted.

King Pyroonak turned to the crowd. 'Point House has lost a child. But it has gained in exchange an Adult; Mungithak!' His formal greeting of the new Adult, palms up, palms down, showed what he was yelling. Mungith was enveloped in Mother Point's hug, while Chooker's yell of delight was lost in the crowd's fresh explosion of cheers and stamping.

9

Silver Doctors rapidly checked Mungith and Chooker, nodding, 'Fine, fine!' and then almost dropped them in eagerness to get back to examine the Giant. Then they spent exhausting hours in the Council Hall among agitated exclamations, demands for details, shrieking arguments. 'We can learn a lot from the monster—Kill it now, before it wrecks Atlantis—No, find out about it first and then kill it— It hasn't hurt anyone, why kill it at all—It could be useful!' The youngsters had never imagined such a commotion was possible in the sedate Council.

Mungith was proud of his discovery, and wanted it to be kept. It hadn't hurt him, he argued. They shouldn't hurt it!

Chooker rather disagreed. She had sensed violence in the Giant's mind, and it was so huge! It was dangerous! But then, it was afraid. Wouldn't she fight for her life too? She didn't know. She was only sure that she didn't want anything more to do with it.

When at last they were sent home, leaving the Council still arguing, they staggered up the path to Point House longing for hot baths and cool drinks. But even there, there was no peace. Worshipful groups gathered round them, demanding the tale again, over and over. Nobody in Point House got much sleep that tide.

At dinner, Mother stood up and rang her bell for silence. 'I've a most important announcement, so pin back your ears!' she told the crowd of eager faces turned to her. 'We knew we had two special events—Prentast's Marriage, and Mungith's Adulthood. Yes, yes, hush, now! But now there are also Mungith's finding of the Giant, and Chooker's splendid courage in helping to rescue her cousin. So . . .' she

71

paused, to keep them in suspense... 'so, we're going to celebrate them all with the finest feast since the Foundation! So eat up, Point, we've work to do!'

As the Hall echoed with applause, she grinned at Chooker. 'New clothes for everyone, even the Nursery. Eh, the teeth we'll be spending! Marvellous!' They laughed together in anticipation. But then Mother's smile faded. 'Chooker, my dear, I have a special task for you.'

Chooker's heart sank. She knew by the tone that she wasn't going to like it.

'The Silvers say the Giant is quite intelligent. Astonishing, for such a brute, but the Little Gods can always surprise us, eh? So the Council decided that the best Sensers should meet every light-tide to examine it, and then we'll decide what to do with it. Now, Distom should go for Point, but he's dark-tide, it would be hard for him, and you know the monster already. So—'

'Eh, no, Mother, please!' Chooker's face was anxious. 'I'm afraid of it. I . . . I hate it! It's so big! It's horrible! Not natural! Not right!'

Mother patted her hand gently but firmly. 'Eh, my dear, but that's a Mother's job, to decide what's right, and what isn't. And it isn't always obvious. You can't—you must not—run away from your duty. Eh? Good. So you'll change into your best kilt, and plait your hair again, it's like a dodo nest, and trot over to Silver House. You'll be junior there, so you mustn't be late. And on your very politest Manners, as I'm sure I don't need to tell you!'

The Silvers had laid two mattresses end to end for the Giant. It lay sleeping, washed and clean, its shin plastered with fresh hardset. Chooker could see it properly for the first time.

It looked almost ordinary except for its huge size. Where it wasn't bruised black or covered with gelset its skin was uneven pinkish cream, almost as light as the Granites, although its head hair was brown, not white. It had short, patchy fur, under its arms and springing through the gelset on its chest, and a red beak of nose poked out below small eyes.

Something bothered Chooker, until she realized what it was. You could tell people's Houses by the colour they shimmered. Points glowed golden; even the Coals, when they washed off the coaldust, gleamed faintly orange. But the poor Giant didn't.

She bowed a greeting to the tall Hunter guarding it, who nodded back. 'Good tide, Point First Daughter.' Her voice was oddly harsh, neither the normal soft tones of the City nor the carrying Hunter shrillness.

The Giant opened its eyes and saw Chooker. After a moment it smiled and raised a hand to her. 'Hiy,' it said.

She made herself smile back. 'Hiy,' she copied it nervously. It grinned wide as a shark.

The guard frowned and hefted her long-handled bronze axe. 'You stay clear of that thing,' she growled. 'It could go crazy any second. Who's to say what monsters will do?'

The woman's face was vaguely familiar. Yellowish skin and black hair, and a greenish sheen—one of the Fish Family, perhaps, or an offshoot? Chooker suddenly remembered the Kelps, in the Battle. Yes, that was it. The guard was the King's sister, the Wilder who had come back to fight for her Family. Now she must have become a Hunter again to earn some teeth. Hem-something. Hemminal. Chooker regarded the woman distrustfully. Prentastal had said she was a thief and a bully. But she'd be on her best Manners now, surely?

'Good tide, Point First Daughter,' a gentle voice murmured. Chooker spun round and bowed deeply to Silver Father, the oldest and most experienced Senser in Atlantis. 'The Giant recognizes you, it seems, though in the mine you were dirty and it was hurt and frightened. But we had realized

73

already that it was intelligent. Yes, yes. Not stupid, no indeed.'

Only twenty-six Houses had a Senser at all—babies with the power were usually adopted by the Houses that specially needed them—and some were too afraid to link minds with the Giant. Tooth, Fire, and Cavy Houses forbade the Sensers of their Houses and all their off-shoots to have anything to do with such an abomination. However, almost all Silvers were Sensers, and several of them came. In the end, over thirty Sensers crowded into the room. The Giant watched keenly as Chooker bowed and bowed to them all. It even bowed a little itself; she felt almost pleased that the brute was showing a proper respect.

Silver Father beamed round at them. 'So many, so many! And so much strength and skill, I know. Shall we try first without the mindreach? Simply with a touch? Eh? It might work.' They nodded agreement. He turned to Chooker, stroked the long white plait of his beard and gazed at her kindly. 'Point First Daughter, the monster knows and likes you, yes, yes... You sit here by and try to keep it calm. Be its friend. If you will?'

'As you wish, Silver Father.' Chooker bowed assent. She had hoped to stay well clear of the monster, out of the way at the back, but you didn't argue with a Father.

Silver Father sat down beside the Giant and took its good hand. All the rest joined hands too, in a long loop right round back to Chooker. 'Take its other wrist, child,' Silver Father told her. She did so, trying not to feel sick at touching it again, and they all concentrated their minds towards the Giant.

It stiffened in fright at the first touch of the joined minds; but Chooker's presence did calm it. After a moment it realized what was happening. Apparently delighted, it organized its ideas to help. It seemed eager to tell them about itself, in pictures of its own world.

74

It—no, he—had a name; touching his chest, he said it aloud; 'Bil Winston Bil' in three bits. To their astonishment, they learned that Bilwinstonbil did not come from the far tunnels, but from Outside. He lived in a hut built on the ice, with other Giants. He tried to explain what they did there, as if it was important. Something about watching rocks grow. Eh, what silliness! But what could you expect from Giants?

He showed them his inside-out picture of the world; a blue ball hanging in black nothingness. Politely, they didn't laugh at his crazy idea that the world travelled round the Great God Rassiyyak, instead of the other way round. Outside was very bright, for half of the time. Yes; that fitted the old tales of the White Tides, and the light of the Great God Rassiyyak, which they could see through the Light Caves that were open up to the ice, or out through Death Gate. Giants all slept when it was dark, Bilwinstonbil declared. The Sensers shook their heads; the City Outside must close down completely for half the day—and in winter, for sixty-tides at a time! How silly!

The Giant's mind passed them pictures of Outside—they managed to tone down the colour. Apparently it wasn't all freezing. It was Giant-size wide and high. The roof shone blue, so high that mist drifted over it, the draughts were very strong, and often water poured down, just as in the legends. Shark Senser pointed out that this proved the Giant was wrong; if the world was surrounded by black, how could the roof be blue? And if Outside had no roof, with ice above it for Rassiyyak to melt, where did the drips fall from?

Wide areas of Outside were covered with green and yellow lichens, some ankle-high, some up to a Giant's waist, many dotted with pretty bright-coloured whorls. In other places, crazy kelp plants stood out in the air, out of water, high above even Giants' heads.

Bilwinstonbil showed them Giants; sixty-sixties of Giants, in queer clothes made of tubes, rushing busily about doing incomprehensible things. He showed them land-boats that floated on an unnatural flat rock that lay in long strips, and moved incredibly fast on round legs at each corner; 'Wheels,' he said aloud, and showed how they worked to carry huge amounts of goods and people across the land Outside. He thought wheelses were very useful, and was surprised that the Sensers didn't know about them.

The Sensers laughed; most of the flat rock in Atlantis was vertical! But the Giant showed them a wheels lifting water, and another working heavy hammers. Ice Senser, whose House supplied hot and cold water to all the Houses and workings, and Chooker whose Family were Smiths, perked up; this was worth learning.

Do you ever fight? Shark Senser asked. Bilwinstonbil almost laughed. He pictured for them Giants fighting; not in proper duels, with paint-rods or knives or harpoons, or even in Battles, but like drunken Wilders. The Sensers winced as they saw great gangs of young Giants fighting with terrible explosive weapons, far worse than spears or bows. And they had no Customs of Battle, so that houses were destroyed.

At that last picture, old Silver Father dropped Bilwinstonbil's hand in horror.

Joining minds was wearying, and this casual destruction was disgusting. No one had the energy to combine again. Silently, tired and shocked, the Sensers left to report to their Families.

Being youngest, Chooker was last to leave, and Silver Father held her back. 'What revolting people!' he said, wearily trying to smile. 'But you must realize, child, that Bilwinstonbil wasn't showing us things he had seen himself, only things he had seen reported. I wonder how... But it can't be like that everywhere. No, indeed.'

He sighed. 'Eh, well. Now that Bilwinstonbil is among civilized people, we must try to educate him. Eh?' He raised an eyebrow at the guard. 'Our best Healers have been working on Mungith and the Giant. The artery is healed, and Mungith is mending nicely, but Giant bone is heavy. It will take several tides for us to join the leg thoroughly. While he's still unsteady, this might be a good time to show him some of Atlantis. What do you think? Eh?'

Hemminal nodded. 'Yuh. He could be tough to handle when he gets his strength back. But don't worry, me and my friends, we'll keep him under control, Silver Father,' she growled.

'Good, good, thank you.' The old man patted Chooker's arm. 'Chooker, my dear, it's a lot to ask of a young girl, but he likes you. Would you be willing to be his guide?'

You didn't argue with a Father. Although Chooker longed to go home to Mother, she bowed assent. 'As you wish, Silver Father. But can he walk far?'

'Eh, eh. A good thought, my dear. H'm.' The old man considered for a moment. 'I'll hire one of the canoes, and you can show him round the main Caverns from the water. '

Chooker brightened; she enjoyed boating. But she didn't want to go alone, not with a Giant and Hemminal. 'Could I ask Mungith to come too, Silver Father?' she asked hopefully. 'Mungithak, I mean. He found the Giant, after all.'

'Why not? Eh, why not, indeed?' Silver Father nodded. 'Excellent, excellent. You run across and get him, eh? While I get the boat organized. And a warm cloak for the Giant— the draughts off the ice can be cold and we can't have him taking a lung fever. No, no.'

If Mungith had thought that as one of the principal guests he'd not have to help prepare the Feast, he soon learned he was wrong. He spent a painful hour while the Point mark was tattooed back and front of his left shoulder, and another tiring period working mentally with a Silver Healer to repair his arm bone and toes. Then he was set to watching the babies while the Nurses sewed new kilts for all the children. Even with all their own work for the Feast, though, his cousins found excuses to visit him, to hear again and again the developing story of how he had boldly tracked and trapped the Giant. He was the hero of the year—of the cycle!

Mother was irritated. Certainly Mungith was due praise, for keeping his wits about him in a terrifying situation, but he was getting far too much attention. His conceit was growing rapidly.

As a result, when Chooker ran in to ask if Mungith could come and help teach the Giant, Mother was quick to agree. 'Eh, of course he may go, feather! It's only right that he should look after the monster that he discovered!' Besides, this would remove him from the hero-worship.

Then she saw Chooker grinning, and realized that the child had caught what she was thinking. Yes, she'd make an excellent Mother!

10

When Chooker saw the Giant upright for the first time, and realized just how huge it was, she couldn't help gaping. Hemminal and a couple of young Silvers were helping it—him—across the quay. His crutches were as tall as she was! He had a whole cavy-felt blanket as a kilt, and three sewn together to make a cloak. He was definitely scary!

They propped the Giant on cushions along one side of a comfortable ten-seater boat, with everyone else on the other side to balance his weight. Chooker had brought Peepik along for the ride, and hugged him for comfort. She was afraid of Bilwinstonbil, his size, his odd smell, his differentness. But he was hurt, and he seemed to like her; and besides Silver Father expected her to care for him. She made herself smile at him. He stared at Peepik, who whiffled wary whiskers and stayed well clear. Chooker wished she could do the same.

Better introduce everybody. She pointed at the Giant and said, 'Bilwinstonbil.'

He grinned, and nodded forwards. 'Bil,' he repeated. 'Bil.'

'Bil?' Mungith snorted. 'He wants to be called by his baby name?'

That annoyed her. Bil, not understanding, was still nodding in a friendly way. Hemminal, in the bow of the canoe, was sneering. She ignored him, pointed to herself, and said, 'Chooker.' Bil repeated it, but had more trouble with Mungithak. Chooker sounded it bit by bit; first the baby name, Mung; then Mungith, the longer name given when a child could walk; and finally the full Adult version, Mungithak. When finally Bil said it correctly, Mungith beamed with pride.

The Wave boatman, climbing to his high seat at the stern post, whistled to his friends to swim into their harness and asked where they wanted to go. Bil stared at the dolphins as if he'd never seen anything like them before. Well, Chooker thought, he probably hadn't.

'Bil would like the dodo farm,' she suggested. She loved the fantastic multi-coloured birds. 'Fancy a dodo race? They'd probably let us do it for free, to show off to the Giant.'

Mungith winced. He did like riding the huge cocks charging round the rocky course, but not today. 'Not with a broken arm,' he said firmly. 'Could Bil walk to the Forges? Or ride?'

'It's much too far!' Chooker wrinkled her nose at him. 'You just want to see if they've finished your new Adult knife, and you know it's unlucky to see it before the day! Isn't that right, Hemminal?'

'Rubbish!' The tall woman snorted rudely. 'Bad luck's just a fool's excuse for bad judgement or clumsiness. Go where you like. Doesn't matter to me.'

What bad Manners! The others glanced at each other in startled silence for a second. Easy to see she'd been a Wilder for years!

Finally, the Wave gently suggested, 'It's almost low tide. We could just get to Big Spout, I think, and then ride the tide back up, right up to the Whirlies if there are fresh dolphins free. And then back down at slack water. We'd be late for light-dinner, but not very.'

At their nods, he whistled again. 'Hold on, people! Here we go!' The dolphins squealed with glee as they whipped the boat out across the City lagoon and into the narrow channel that led to the maze of water caves. The Giant yelped in alarm. Everyone did, first time through. They all laughed, even Bil.

Mungith tried to teach the Giant. 'Boat . . . head . . . hand.' Bil tried to repeat the words, but he had difficulty with anything longer than three syllables. After a while, Mungith gave up. 'He's a dull!' he complained, sitting back in disgust. 'You try, Chook!'

Chooker jumped. 'Me?'

'Yes, you!' He nodded in a lordly way. 'You've touched his mind before, in the mine and in Silver House. Do it again, and try to teach him something useful.'

'What, alone? No!'

He sniffed. 'I thought you'd want to help. But if you can't be bothered . . .'

She puffed in annoyance. 'That's not it, and you know it! His mind isn't like ours. He's . . . he's sickening. Well, upsetting, anyway. I'd rather try to read a shark. No!' No, she couldn't!

Peepik squeaked as she squeezed him too hard, and she had to soothe him. Bil smiled tentatively, and reached out a finger. Mungith grinned expectantly. Peepik sniffed the finger, but didn't bite it. That was unusual, with strangers; Chooker often had to apologize for his bad Manners. Bil didn't know how honoured he was. She made a face at Mungith.

By now they were running past the dodo farm. Bil heaved himself up to gape at the huge, brilliant cocks waddling up and down the slope, some in immense, noble dignity, others squabbling round the dull brown hens. The Wave whistled to the dolphins to slow down, and Chooker grinned. 'Eh, I knew he'd like them,' she boasted. 'Dodo,' she told Bil. 'Dodo.'

He nodded, pointed eagerly and repeated something three times. 'He knows them,' Mungith commented. 'That must be his word for them. But what a silly short word!'

Chooker rolled her eyes. 'Maybe Giants are too stupid to remember long words.'

At the lock where the tunnels towards the coal-mines joined the main flow, Mungith acted to Bil that that was where he had fallen through the rock.

Hemminal growled, 'Don't waste your time. You were right, he's a dull.'

'No, he isn't. Look, he's nodding. He understands almost as well as a real person,' Mungith objected. The Giant was going to be so useful, once he'd learned to speak! And everyone who saw him would remember who had found him!

Bil's mouth was twisted. He pointed to himself and the boat, over the lock and along the passage. He repeated the action several times.

'He wants to go out again,' Chooker said. She shook her head at the Giant.

'Out? Outside, you mean? Why?' Mungith demanded.

She puffed in exasperation. 'It's his home! Wouldn't you want to go home?'

'Well, yes,' Mungith admitted. 'But I'm not a Giant. He's far better off here than Outside. Besides, he can't go, he's mine. Or the Coals'. Eh, talk of the Coals, look!'

A massive team of ten dolphins and a dozen paddlers was heaving a laden coal barge out of the lock, ready to run up to the City with the tide. Mungith called and waved, for he recognized one of the paddlers. 'Hey, Giffaral! Greetings! How's the tawch doing?' he yelled.

Giffaral glanced over at him and Bil, and snorted. 'Dead,' she called back. 'Only lived half a tide. Useless rubbish!' She spat derisively into the water, and turned back to work.

Deflated, Mungith sat back. Dead? It had seemed such a wonderful thing. So much light, so easy to control. Disappointing. But not his fault, of course.

In Big Spout Cave, they tucked the canoe into the sheltered inlet where the inrush wouldn't overturn it. People often came here for picnics on holidays, but this tide they had it to themselves. The Wave dived in, and the dolphins bobbed round him, whistling gleefully and peering curiously at the stranger. Bil reached a nervous hand to scratch the head of the nearest, smiling when it angled its head to let him rub its bulge. Animals seemed to like him, Chooker thought. Maybe he wasn't all bad.

82

'We've timed it well,' the Wave said. 'Not long to wait.'

When Chooker unpacked the mid-tide snacks Mother had given them, Mungith grabbed one of the stuffed hard-boiled dodo eggs. 'What spice is it? Yay, my favourite!' She beamed at pleasing him. Hemminal took one with a grunt, ripped off the wrapping and bit into it as if she hadn't eaten for a ten-tide. The Wave didn't want any, of course. Waves only ate raw fish, like their dolphins. Bil took a big half-egg, as large as even his two cupped hands, and slowly unwrapped the thin kelp sheet from it, shaking his head in wonderment.

Peepik wandered off to sniff at Hemminal, who flicked him aside. Peepik bit her, and was swiped towards the water. Chooker dived to catch him before he fell in; the dolphins might well have snapped him up. She glared at Hemminal, who glared right back. 'You keep that rat off me!' she growled. 'Or he'll end up as supper!' Chooker gulped. Wilders did steal and eat pets.

Suddenly behind them there was a deep, echoing belch. Bil jumped round.

'Eh! The tide!' Mungith yelled. He pointed to the hole in the rocks, an arm-span above the pool. Bil stared, puzzled, and then shouted, startled, as the first gout of foam poured from the hole; then a gush, a jet of water roaring right across the cave.

'Big Spout! It can overturn boats!' Mungith bawled, waving his hands to show boats spinning and sinking under the torrent. Bil nodded, and made movements with his own hands, something about the water, and then under the water, twisting along.

'He's trying to show us he understands how the water comes in through the rock!' Chooker suggested.

Mungith sneered. 'Don't be silly—how would a monster know about that kind of thing?'

Bil started to laugh.

Suspiciously, Hemminal hefted her axe, but Bil just sat and laughed louder. He stared round, holding up his half-eaten egg, pointing to them and himself, to Peepik, to the boat rising with the rising water, to the Wave and his dolphins frolicking in the cold, fresh rush of the tide-spout, gesturing all round, shouting something in his own language, laughing more and more helplessly until they couldn't help smiling with him, although they didn't know what was so funny.

'He can't believe it!' Chooker realized what was happening. 'It's like a dream. He's just happy at being with real people and seeing all our wonders! Like us meeting the Little Gods!'

They joined the poor, ignorant Giant in his laughter.

As soon as the level rose above the inrush, enough for it to be safe to move the boat, they headed back up-tide, past the seaweed farms with the eel and octopus pools, and the wide kelp lagoon where seals came through an underwater crack somewhere to shelter from the long dark Outside. They had a smooth, fast run right up through the complex of caverns. Bil was lost in admiration as relays of dolphins came at the Wave's whistle to take up the harness loops and speed them on through the zig-zag of many-coloured caves, pink, green and orange, lilac, purple and cream, white, yellow, greeny-blue, some flickering or flowing in waves of two or three colours as warm and cold draughts whispered along the rocks.

They reached the top cave, where the water roared away to Outside in vast whirlpools, just before high tide. The boat stopped at the second-last cave. Dolphins would romp among the Whirlies as happily as in the inrush, but Waves never brought their beloved friends up there. Any that adventured too far into the current could be sucked down and badly hurt or lost.

Lurching on his crutches, Bil climbed with the others through the tunnel to the wide, low top cave. It was near the ice, and the air was chilly. He shivered in the cold blue glow, in spite of his cloak. Even Mungith was subdued here, in the roar of the whirlpools where the God lived.

Four boats, red-flagged for funerals, had followed them. In turn, three long red bundles were carried up on the shoulders of the men of their Families, laid on the raft by the rocks and pushed into the current. At the end of its chain, the raft jerked and tilted; the bodies tipped off, to sink at once into the huge central swirl. 'Go to Beliyyak in safety, and return to life soon!' their cousins and brothers called. 'The Little Gods watch over you—but not too closely!' They tossed strings of teeth after the bodies, to pay the God for a speedy passage back to life. Chooker, Mungith, and even Hemminal clapped and stamped gently in respect. Bil frowned.

Chooker frowned back at him. What did Giants do with their dead, then? Eat them?

Then Up Flat Triangle Mother carried in a red-wrapped baby, weakly whimpering.

Bil was puzzled. Mungith tried to explain why the baby was there, but hands weren't enough. 'Ay, come on, Chooker!' he exclaimed in exasperation. 'You try! Please!'

The trip had gone so well that Chooker gave in to Mungith's urging and took Bil's hand. To her pleasure, he understood and cleared his mind for her. Contact wasn't too hard.

As it happened, Chooker had been present as First Daughter when Triangle Mother had asked Point Mother's advice. She imaged for Bil the baby's damaged spine. *Never sit up, never walk or hunt. Pain, constant pain.* That was hard enough, but she tried to go further. *Male spirits have to come up from the City Cavern to Beliyyak here, to start their next life. Men know the way, but a baby would be lost, crying in pain forever round the City. Mother sends him safe to the God now, before he dies, in love, to start his next life at once. Better life next time.* Thinking such difficult, abstract ideas was very difficult, and she didn't know how much Bil could understand. She wiped sweat from her face, in spite of the cold.

Bil was horrified. He felt only a useless and, Chooker thought, merciless sympathy for the child. *If you love it, you can't kill it!* he insisted.

We're not killing it! We do love it, so we can't make it suffer! Chooker retorted.

Triangle Mother knelt to lay the baby on the funeral raft. 'Go safely in love—'

With a cry of distress, Bil lunged forward over the rocks, shouting, 'Noh! Noh!'

Grunting in pure pleasure, Hemminal tripped him and held him with a foot on his bad leg. Everyone turned to stare at the bad Manners; Wilder behaviour!

Red-faced, Mungith bowed apology to the mourners, and the raft was thrust out into the current. They all watched the tiny bundle tip and vanish in the blue swirl. 'Noh!' Bil whispered.

Chooker was furious. How could he try to stop them helping the child? How dared he? He was only a Giant.

11

About Bil's shocking behaviour, Mother said sensibly that you couldn't expect a Giant to understand Custom—and at least he was trying to be kind, even if in a stupid way, not vicious or destructive. 'I have an idea, feather!' she exclaimed. 'You ask Silver Father if the Giant can come to the Feast tomorrow. We'll all be thrilled to get a good look at him, and I'm sure Silver House will be glad to let someone else feed him for once!' She was speaking over her shoulder, already moving towards the next person who wanted to speak to her.

Chooker didn't want Bil at her Feast! Well, Mung's Feast, and Prentast's. Eh, well. You didn't argue with a Mother.

At Silver House next day, Chooker regarded Bil distrustfully. Hemminal, on guard again, nodded to her but didn't speak. Chooker didn't mind; this was another person she didn't like.

Today, Bil greeted the Sensers eagerly. He wanted to show them how skilful his people were at medicine, saving people with terrible injuries and illnesses.

Diffidently, Chooker interrupted to tell how Bil had reacted to the baby's funeral the day before. The Sensers were pleased. This kindness was a good side of Giants.

Bil's pleasure at the approval was vivid in their minds. He had obviously been planning what to show them, and now expanded his thoughts, much clearer today, showing Giant Doctors doing surgery, like Heart House. *See—we cure growths and accidental damage, split palates and holes in hearts.* Silver Father and Heart Senser were almost cheering. *Faults like birthmarks and extra limbs and fingers—*

Chooker jumped. Heart Senser froze. Drop Senser sat up tall on his stool. 'Faults?' In their disbelief they all spoke aloud.

Why, yes, Bil thought in surprise. *Anything abnormal...*

Young Heart Senser had just paid two full strings of teeth to have shadows tattooed under the wide red patches all over her, the proud birthmark of her House, to make them stand out in relief from her white skin. She had a particularly striking one on her face. Faults?

Drop Senser shoved back his pink cloak to show off his under-left arm. Third and fourth arms were usually weak, and not much use to heavy-work Houses like Point or Granite. However, Drop and Crystal Houses, who made glassware and jewellery, or Lace, who specialized in fine sewing, found them most useful, and were eager to adopt any such baby. No one with only two arms could be Lace Mother. Remove the special arm? Never!

Chooker had five fingers on each hand, like most Coppers and Points, and many Triangles. Fish House and its off-shoots often had more, and an extra thumb. A few spares were a good thing. You could easily lose a finger or two to a moray eel or a slipping hammer; if you only had four to start with you could end up in trouble. Many Waves had only three long fingers and toes, but had useful webs between them, to swim with their dolphins. Abnormal?

Bil felt the shock, and hesitated. Then, as the insult and outrage grew, his mind tried to run away. They wouldn't let him. Furious, they demanded *Why do you think that? How dare you?* At last he tugged loose from their hands, hid his face and sat shuddering at the attack.

The Sensers gazed at each other in amazement.

Slowly, the comments came, and the arguments spread. 'Giants are all alike—What a narrow idea of what is normal, what is acceptable—They even dislike different colours of skins—They cut bits off babies till they match, how vile!—But babies with less than normal arms or legs, they care for them—Or with dead minds! Disgusting!—Or the ones with terrible diseases, or accidents. They look after them with great care—Yes, for years, until they die slowly—They don't let them go on to a better life next time—They don't believe that—So? They make them wretched by not accepting them, and then keep them alive to suffer!'

'Giants are crazy!' Shark Senser's screech stilled the din. He stared round the room, very agitated. 'What if he tries to bring his Customs here? He tried to stop the baby's return to new life yesterday. What if he tries to cut off Drop Senser's arm, or my tail, or Chooker's spare fingers? What if he convinces any foolish youngsters that his way is right? He must be killed, like a mad rat! He is dangerous!'

'No, no, not if we keep him under proper control,' Silver Father argued. 'What-ifs are not a good reason for doing anything.'

'You'll take that risk? Eh, that's your choice, but you can't make everyone else take it!'

'No, no, Shark Senser, I agree we must be careful. Take precautions.' The old man's white plait wagged as he nodded firmly. 'Yes, indeed. Every care. Bil must always be guarded. Every moment. Hemminal—will you and your friends see to that? Eh, yes, good, good. And no one may talk to him alone, to prevent his madness taking hold of anyone's mind. That way he should be no danger. No, no.' He looked round. 'Are we agreed?'

Slowly, they agreed. No one wanted to lose the chance to get more good ideas, like wheelses. But equally, no one wanted the Giant's crazy ideas to spread.

They all turned to look at Bil.

He was studying them carefully. He gazed at Pearl's short fawn fur and Arrow's jutting lower canine teeth; at Drop's extra arm; at Shark's long tail, its tip flicking in agitation, and at the great russet mane flowing over Slash's shoulders and back; at the extra fingers or large ears or plaited eyebrows or multi-coloured skin; at kindly Silver Father's single eye.

Now they understood his earlier recoil. They had thought it was wonder and awe, but it was loathing.

Even as they watched him, he shrank in on himself.

Silver Father was smiling. 'Can't you feel it?' he murmured. 'He is changing. Yes, yes. The disgust is still there—but it's turning to disgust of himself. He is not bad—just wrong. Badly taught. He is realizing that people can be different, and still be people. Yes, yes.'

Suddenly they all jumped as Bil grabbed Chooker's hand, and reached out towards Silver Father again. 'Let go!' Chooker gasped, and jerked free.

His eyes swung back to her. 'Chooker . . . Chooker!' He beckoned to her.

'He wants to tell us something. Something important. We should listen.' Silver Father sat down again beside the Giant. 'Eh, please, all of you, join us. Chooker . . . please?'

Chooker gulped. But you didn't argue with a Father—and Bil didn't look violent. Upset, yes, but not threatening. She made herself sit down again and gingerly lay her hand on his wrist.

Bil looked at the five small fingers, and bit his lip; and suddenly his mind burst open to them. They sensed a new respect for them, just before his mind went off on what they soon realized was a glimpse of Outside history.

He showed them that killing, ruthless killing, was part of life Outside. He showed men dressed in metal, riding on animals huger than even the biggest riding rats, killing even babies. He showed people being starved or shot or poisoned or clubbed to death, and dropped into huge pits or stuffed into furnaces. He showed explosions, like gas in the mines, that killed whole Cities of people.

Desperately, Bil warned them, *Stay away!* Giants' fires belched poisonous smoke, and they carelessly poured poison into the streams and the sea, and on to the land. Every small nation of people who had ever met Giants had suffered. Their land had been taken, by force or lies. They had been slaughtered, hunted like cockroaches, or had died of disease—sometimes deliberately spread. And there was no way to fight; Giants had gas bombs and flamethrowers that would reach to the furthest tunnels. *Stay away from Outside!*

Stop! Old Silver Father could take no more of it. He broke the link. Arrow Senser was sick. Several of the others were in tears. Frozen with horror, Chooker stared at Bil.

The Giant was trembling with exhaustion, sobbing on his stone bench, sweating, white and shaken himself by the effort he had put into the meeting of minds.

Gradually, the Sensers recovered.

'They'll kill us. We're different, we're small and odd-shaped to them, and compared to them and their weapons we're weak. So they'll kill us.' Panting in fear and fury, Shark Senser glared round at them all, among nods and mutters. 'So we must kill him!'

'But he warned us!' Chooker protested before she had time to think about Manners. She blushed as they stared at her, but made herself go on. 'He's trying to help us! We can't kill him!'

Slowly, Silver Father nodded. 'Eh, yes, child. I believe you are right.' He gazed round at the others. 'What a puzzle—and what is the answer? Which is the normal action for Giants? Eh? The evil, against which he warned us—or the good, that shows in their care for the sick, and in his warning against his own kind? Think about it. Eh, think. They can't all be totally destructive.'

'If even a few are, it's too big a risk!' Shark Senser insisted.

'We must destroy him!' Pearl Senser shouted.

Cat Senser agreed with Chooker. 'It's not so simple. If all his people are so evil, it seems uncanny that we are lucky enough to be found by the only good one. Try again, please, Silver Father. Find out the answer to this puzzle.'

Few of the other Sensers would join the link this time. After another long minute's contact, Silver Father sighed. 'He says that few Giants are really evil, but many are thoughtless or callous. And then, Giants don't have Sensers, like us, to check whether people are good-minded or bad. So, the few who are greedy and ruthless, ready to lie or cheat or do anything to become their Kings and Queens, are often the ones who do. The good Giants can't find out the bad ones until too late. So we would be destroyed, he says, before the good ones knew about it.'

Silver Father raised his hands against the growing uproar of argument. 'Eh, my friends, we're all upset. Naturally. What we have seen would upset Osiriyyak Himself. Yes, yes, indeed. Not since the destruction of the world have we ever imagined such horrors. We are not fit to make good judgements now. No, no. At least, I know that I am not.' His hands were shaking, and he rubbed them together as if to warm them. 'No, indeed. Tomorrow, when we are calmer, we can talk to Bil again, and consider our report to the full Council. It will decide the matter. It is not entirely our decision. For which I am indeed thankful. Eh, yes.'

He sighed. 'My friends, this may be the most important moment in the history of Atlantis since the Foundation. We must not act in foolish rage, or fear, or equally foolish rashness or hope, but only in good sense and honour and reason, for the sake of Atlantis. Let the Little Gods watch over us now.' He smiled slightly. 'But not too closely.'

12

Whatever was happening in Silver House, Point House could think of nothing but the Feast.

Still slightly shaky after his Farewell Feast at Drop House the tide before, Crosstenak arrived for his Wedding. At the end of the terrace he hugged his brothers, who had escorted him—Roof brats liked to throw dirt at the long white hooded cloak of a Bridegroom—and walked along to Point House. He turned to wave, and slipped in by the end door through the kitchen to the Men's Room. Everyone carefully avoided seeing him, for the cloak made him 'invisible'. By Custom, no one should be officially aware that he was here except the Groom's Friend. Today, that was Mungithak.

Mungith had spent half a tide in the Men's Room, getting ready. Now the last men had gone into the hall, he had peace to admire himself in the long silver mirror. Yes, he looked good. Mother had made him a new Adult tunic in sleek black sealskin, slanting from a deep point below his left knee, upwards to the single broad strap on his right shoulder that displayed the new House tattoo on his left. And the enormous fan of black hair above his right eye—he ran a gentle finger up the edge—eh, really stylish. And it wouldn't collapse this time!

'In love with yourself, bonny boy?' Crosstenak commented drily behind him.

Mungith started, but grinned without turning. 'Jealous, eh? I didn't hear you come in, the cloak muffled the clinking— eh, what a wealth of teeth! You're very nearly late—I was starting to think you'd cried off!' He smiled, oh-so-modestly. 'I was just checking my hair. It's set so hard I don't know how they'll cut it when I go down to Hunters' Hall tomorrow!'

Crossten snorted. 'Don't worry, they'll manage. They're used to it. One swish, and—' He mimed the swing of a long knife just above Mungith's scalp, and the high fan of hair tumbling to the floor. 'Doesn't matter whether you want a boat, or to go rat-hunting like Motor. No team would take you on looking like a geyser!' He saw the waver in Mungith's smile, and slapped the young man's shoulder comfortingly. 'No, you look fine.'

'So do you. Honestly!' Mungith assured him. 'How does the wedding tunic always make men look taller? The length of plain white, I suppose. And then the wig, too.'

Crossten eased the pillar of white hair off his forehead. 'It's giving me a headache. I'll be glad when it's all over and I can take it off.'

Mungith smiled at him, thinking for once about another person's feelings. Although Crossten was an experienced Harpooner, master of his boat, and had already been made welcome by the whole House, he was fidgeting and twitching, his festooned teeth chittering nervously. It was always hard for a man who married outside his House, coming alone among strangers. If—no, when—he married Chooker, Mungith was glad that he wouldn't have to do it. 'Calm down! You look as if you were going to fight a school of killer whales.'

'I'd rather, any day!' Crossten stretched and shook himself to loosen his muscles.

'It can't be that bad,' Mungith chuckled. 'Prentast won't eat you. Well, probably not!' He peeked out round the curtain. 'They're nearly ready. Just the Giant to come.'

All in their Feast finery, Point Family were settling into their places. The walls and roof of the wide Hall glowed golden, with bright mosaics of blue and white, copper and black chevrons along the walls and all up the pillars. Plaited chains of specially bright glow-ropes criss-crossed the ceiling and reflected from the burnished copper chevrons inset round the edges of the slate tables. At the top table, across the end of the Hall, would sit Point Mother and Father and the guests of honour. The four long tables below them were for the Married Couples, the Men, the Women, and the Children in their new bronze codskin tunics, with their Nurses. At the far end the Mica band were tuning up quietly.

They all murmured and rattled in admiration as Mother appeared in a shimmering swirl of copper mussel-silk lace. Distom, greeting her formally with touching palms, loudly tutted disapproval. 'Where are the teeth to come from, Mother, to pay for all these frills and fripperies? Do you think we just go hunting for them?' he complained. Everyone laughed at the old joke.

Mother, who was also his mother, sniffed at him and appealed to the whole House. 'Eh, what a skinflint! You'll just have to bargain harder!' The laugh grew; under Distom's management, Point could well afford the expense.

The children on watch at the door scurried in. 'The Giant! It's coming!'

'Calmly, now!' Mother warned sternly over the excited stir. 'No squawks, or staring, or rude remarks—this isn't a Roof House! Manners, please!'

In spite of Mother's instruction, they all gasped. The chains of glow-ropes threatened to strangle the Giant if he stood straight. Peeking round the curtain, Mungith thought Bil looked like a miner in a tunnel, his crutches sprawling wide, crouching down while trying to keep his head up and look round. Mother preened at his obvious amazement and admiration.

'Greetings to Point House!' Hemminal's voice had softened only slightly in the days since her return, but she bowed politely deep. 'May we enter?'

Point Mother stepped forward, hands outstretched. 'Be welcome to our feast.' She touched palms with Hemminal, up and down, while Distom greeted the Giant.

95

'Be welcome, Bil.' It took considerable courage for Distom to touch the Giant's hands; he scarcely reached Bil's waist. But he radiated welcome and friendship, and felt curiosity and wonder in return; there was no threat here.

Everyone wanted to touch hands with Bil, and it was quite a while before he reached the top table, where a stone bench had been set for him in case he was too heavy for the bone basketwork stools the rest used. He plumped down on the cushions with a puff of relief, and laid down the crutches. The Silvers had made him a kilt of their own special grey sealskin, plain but good quality, so that he'd not disgrace himself and them. Beside him, in a rat-leather kilt and belt in the vivid Kelp green, blue, and gold swirls, Hemminal set her axe lovingly by her knee.

Distom exchanged a glance with Mother. Ready? Right. He nodded to the Mica conductor to begin the fanfares. Mother nodded to the children at the doors of the Men's and Women's Rooms, who swept back the curtains.

'Here we go!' Crossten drew a deep breath and jerked his head. 'You're on first.'

Mungith's throat was dry. He swallowed, straightened, and walked out into the Hall.

From the Women's Room, Chooker led out her sister. Chooker's hair had been scented, and set for the first time ever into the wide fan that was the fashion just now. Chevrons were painted on her shoulder, and she was laced into a new formal calf-length tunic of gleaming golden salmon-leather that showed off her pendant. She knew she looked pretty, but she was a shadow beside Prentastal.

The Point wedding gown, worn by every Point Bride, was a glimmering tabard of tiny diamonds of mother-of-pearl, beaded with chevrons in jet and copper right round the sloping shoulder and the pointed hems of the skirt's panels, and the ribbons at shoulder and hip. The white Bride's wig with glittering pearl, copper, and jet ornaments woven into it had been dressed high as a fountain, almost touching the lights as Prentastal moved forward, tall and stately.

They all four bowed to the Family. Everyone clapped.

In the centre of the Hall, Mother and Distom were waiting. The little man's face was composed, but a great warmth reached out to welcome and hearten them. He beckoned forward Chooker and Mungith first, and raised a hand for silence.

'Mungith, son of Point Adults Vustorak and Krantowal, went into the mines for his Adult Trial, and spent ten tides there. He acted with great courage and good sense, even during a rock-fall. When he found the Giant—' all eyes flicked for an instant to Bil, watching fascinated—'he remained calm, and brought this huge monster safely back. The King declared that Atlantis is proud to accept him as an Adult.'

Distom turned Mungith to face the Family. 'Point House, I introduce to you all a new Adult of this House, with all the rights and duties of that position. May the Little Gods watch over him—but not too closely. Be welcome, Mungithak!'

Everyone joined the chant: 'Mung-Mungith-Mungithak! Mungithak! Mungithak! Mungithak! Mungithak!' The name was shouted faster and faster, speeding up till it dissolved into cheering and stamping applause.

Sayvallak, the Chief Smith, stepped forward holding a sharkskin scabbard, attached to a copper-coloured leather shoulder sash. Sternly, Sayvallak drew out a long blade. Silence fell again as he held it up for all to admire the chevrons of silver wire inlaid in the dark, tough bronze. 'This is your Adult knife, Mungithak. Wear it safely, and use it with courage and honour and good sense!' Sayvallak slid the blade home and slipped the sash over Mungith's head. The scabbard banged his left knee, long and heavy and awkward and wonderful!

As Mungith was hugged by Distom and by Point Mother, his heart was thudding painfully. He was exalted, higher than the Roof with delight, drunk with pride and happiness, as he started his rounds of the tables to be greeted by everyone with his full Adult name for the first time.

After a while, when hands were starting to turn numb, Point Mother waved for calm. 'Hush, now, my children!' She beckoned Chooker to step shyly forward beside her. 'You all know how my own child Chooker, Point First Daughter, went into the mines without any warning or preparation to help find Mungithak when he was trapped. Even though she knew the roof was unsafe! The Queen, and the whole Council, agree that this deed of exceptional bravery deserves an exceptional reward. It is decided that Chooker may declare herself an Adult whenever she feels herself ready, without having to go through another Trial. It's a very rare privilege. Isn't that wonderful?' She beamed down at Chooker. 'The Little Gods have been watching over you!'

Linking with Mungith's exultation, Chooker had thought that nothing could add to her joy. But now, the glowing pride of Distom, her Mother, and the whole Family raised her to a new peak of happiness. Nothing could ever be as wonderful again!

The cheering slowly died away, and people started blowing on their hands to cool them. Distom and Point Mother beckoned Prentastal and Crosstenak forward, with Chooker and Mungith behind them.

Distom bowed and smiled to Crosstenak. 'Who are you, and why do you come?'

'Father Point, I am Crosstenak, Adult of Drop House. I come to join Point House.'

'Why should Point accept you?'

Deliberately, Crosstenak shivered. The tassels of teeth that swung from his arms and legs, and covered his whole body, chittered loudly in the silence. 'I bring teeth. I bring my skills and my strength. I bring love for Prentastal, Adult of Point House.'

Mother bowed to him. 'Then you are welcome.' She turned to her daughter. 'Prentastal, Adult of Point House, do you wish to become the wife of Crosstenak, Adult of Drop House?'

Prentastal's voice was clear and calm. 'Yes, I do.' she smiled to Crosstenak.

It was Distom's turn. 'Crosstenak, Adult of Drop House, do you wish to become the husband of Prentastal, Adult of Point House?'

One eyebrow raised, the short, sturdy man glanced up at the tall woman beside him, and kept them all in suspense for a moment as if considering the matter. Chooker suddenly had to suppress a fit of giggles. What if Crosstenak shocked them all by saying, 'No!' With all her force, she thought, *Yes! Say yes!* at him. Grins spread round the Hall; if Crosstenak had the nerve to play jokes during his wedding, he'd be a lot of fun! He finally declared, 'Yes, I do.'

Distom controlled his twitching lips, and turned to the House. 'Does anyone here know of any reason why these two Adults should not marry?'

Again, Crosstenak's eyebrow twitched. Chooker knew he was wondering if anyone ever did interrupt.

Distom reached across to lift Prentastal's hand, while Mother took Crosstenak's. They joined all four hands together. 'Crosstenak,' he said, 'will you promise before the assembly of Point House, and Beliyyak, God of men, as witnesses, to care for Prentastal and her children for all the rest of your life?'

Crosstenak turned to his bride. 'Yes. I will. In love.' Prentastal's face flamed with pleasure at the firmness and sincerity of his tone.

Mother's voice was stern. 'Prentastal, will you promise before the assembly of Point House, and Bastiyyal, Goddess of women, as witnesses, to bear Crosstenak's children, and care for him and them for all of your life?'

Prentastal's smile was glorious. 'Yes, I will. In love.'

Mother and Distom stepped back, smiling, releasing their hands, leaving them alone and hand-fast in the centre of the Hall. 'I, Point Mother, speak for Point House. I accept Crosstenak as the husband of our daughter Prentastal. From this moment he is a son of Point House.'

Distom smiled at Prentastal, 'I, Point Father, speak for Point House. Prentastal is now wife of our new son Crosstenak. May they be happy and prosperous.'

They spoke together. 'May the Little Gods watch over them—'

And the Family chorused, laughing, 'But not too closely!'

As the cheering erupted again, the couple hugged. Mungith giggled and exchanged a grin with Chooker as both newly-weds had to shove their wigs straight again, before they started on the round of the tables, greeting every member of the Family.

A Bride didn't wear her teeth to her wedding, as everyone had a gift to drape over her arms. Children gave one or two; Mother, Distom, and the older men and women gave whole tassels. Every so often, Prentastal had to unload them to Chooker, to put in a huge basket laid in the centre of the Hall; the couple were so popular that it filled to overflowing. When they had been all round, and settled at last in their seats at the top table, it took two people to carry the basket off to their cubicle.

At a signal from Mother, helpers from the Triangle Houses brought in the Feast. Bil gasped. Mouths watering at the delicious smells, everyone sighed in delight as the slate table-tops vanished under the dishes.

Six roast dodos displaying all their brilliant feathers, on beds of crispy black laver-weed; a whole roast porpoise and a baked shark; piled baskets of crunchy deep-fried ratlings in batter; fish and shellfish of three dozen varieties, squid broiled in its own ink, smoked eels and spiced fish roes;

huge roasts of cavy; mountains of dodo and petrel eggs; tiny cavy and rat cheeses by the dozen; six kinds of seaweed; jars of the Yeasts' special cream; jugs of the Hoops' finest ales—every House in the City, it seemed, had been raided. Relays of cooks had laboured non-stop for six tides at the big House ovens, and the long rows of Point yeast-vats had been scraped to the dregs, as every cook in the Family helped with the main dishes and then added their own specialities to the spread—sweet and spicy cakes and pastries and puddings and omelettes and biscuits, nibbles and spreads and pickles, hot pies and sausages, iced creams and jellies.

Yes, Mother thought complacently. Atlantis would talk of this Feast for a cycle!

The Mica Band started to play quietly; dancing would start later, weapons displays, a juggler from Sea-urchin House, a cock-fight, acrobats and a contortionist from Squid House, even a duel that had been put off till the feast, to allow betting—not a serious one to the death or even to first blood, of course, to spoil the fun; just first three touches. Most money was on the tall Sea Spider, whose height should make the difference against a short Lace, even if the Lace had four arms to hold the long, whippy paint-rods that showed touches. But for the moment everyone was too busy eating to do more than listen.

At the top table, Mungith blinked; the glows were really very bright. Uncomfortably bright. The drumming was echoing through his head. Even the harps were loud. Crosstenak grinned over at him. 'Headache?' he asked. 'Me too. It's the wig, I think. And the heat in here.'

Mungith sniffed. 'More likely a hangover from your Farewell party last night!' But yes, it could be having to balance the elaborate hair-do that was giving him a stiff neck. He didn't feel at all well, but he'd not admit it, not for the world! He rubbed his forehead.

Chooker was frowning at him. Beyond her, so was Bil, pausing in his enjoyment of a spicy pie. Mungith made himself grin cheerfully, and they grinned back, dismissing their moment's unease.

13

Within six tides, an epidemic had struck Atlantis.

The tide after the feast, Mungith was hot and restless, shivering, aching in every joint, wincing from light, his nose blocked. He was certainly in no state to go down to Hunter's Halls.

He was moved from his hammock to a bed in the Sick Room and a Silver was called. Her mind calmed him while with her pocket lens she studied his blood and nose-drips, but she shook her head doubtfully. 'I don't see anything... Eh, well, it's a kind of fever, so we'll treat it that way for now. Ice packs and cool baths, but don't let him chill. A fever powder in warm milk every tide. Sea-squirt poultices to ease the aching joints, a pain-stop pill under his tongue. That nose-clear resin the Loops make for the Coals—keep a stick smoking here all the time. Plenty to drink. And keep the children away from him, in case they catch it.' She frowned down at Mungith. 'He's not the only one. One of our men feels much the same, and just as I was leaving, an urgent call came in from Coal House—and you know how Coals pride themselves on being tough.'

Chooker, seated beside Mungith's bed to soothe him, glanced up. 'Was it for people from the mine where Mung did his Trial?'

'I believe—yes, it could be!' The Silver's jaw dropped. 'And Joorull—eh, yes, he was the one who went out to that call. Bil. You think this sickness may come from Outside?' She seemed more interested than shocked.

Chooker shivered. 'Something he once told us—this illness might not bother him, he might not even know he had it, but someone who'd never met it before—'

'Wouldn't be immune. Eh, of course!'

'He's brought in something that could kill us all?' Point Mother stiffened. 'Bil? He's done this? Eh, Bastiyyal take him! The cockroach! The hagfish!'

'He didn't mean to!' Chooker protested. 'He didn't know he was coming here!'

Mother wasn't listening; she had other cares. 'Distom—he went to the meeting this tide, he insisted, he'll be touching Bil—and everyone did at the Feast—eh, Bastiyyal watch over us—and you, feather, you've been with that monster even more than Mung. Are you feeling all right?'

Chooker sighed. 'Not really, Mother. My bones are aching.'

Mother turned white. 'Bed. Now.' She turned to the door. 'That Bil! We must kill it, at once, now, before it gives this illness to the whole City. I'll send out warning, call the Council—'

The Silver caught her arm. 'Mother Point! Calm down! If your First Daughter's idea is correct—and we don't know yet if it is—that still doesn't mean that killing the Giant would help!'

'Mother!' Chooker whispered. 'Mother, if this is an Outside illness, Bil might—' Her throat was so sore she had to stop, but the Silver picked up her thought.

'Of course! He may know a cure!' She rushed out, while Chooker winced at the sudden noise and movement. When Mother sent a boy running for her bedroll, she was glad to strip off her kilt, wrap the soft quilt round herself and crawl into bed.

Mungith felt sure he was dying. He almost hoped he was. He had never been really ill before, and it terrified him. Every muscle ached. In his fever, the room fuzzed and fused, ballooned and twisted round him; his head and his feet shrank and stretched, tiny and huge, near and far. He moaned helplessly. Someone gave him a drink, and cooled his forehead with an ice-pack. But it wasn't Chooker, or Mother; where were they?

Chooker was tossing in the next bed, feeling with her cousin, heaving and moaning in reaction to Mungith's pains until the Nurses insisted she took a sleep drink and at last she settled. Mungith, who had been reacting to her in turn, calmed as well.

Mother was busy. All her usual dramatic over-acting set aside, she called all the Adults of her tide to an emergency meeting. 'Now, we've no time for hysterics and flapping,' she told them sternly. 'If Bil brought this sickness, it could spread right through Atlantis. Terrible, eh, yes, but my first concern is Point House. We've been in contact with Bil for longer than any other House except the Coals, and they're sick. We could be next, within a tide or two.'

They puffed in dismay, but no one wasted time arguing or exclaiming.

'Do you remember what old Mother Traxant did—or rather didn't do—in that dreadful dysentery epidemic thirty years ago? When a quarter of the House died of panic and neglect, not just disease? Eh, I'll not let that happen again! We'll prepare now. Just in case. Let the other half rest—they'll take over in their tide. We can get started.' They nodded determined agreement.

'If the Sick Room isn't big enough, we can move the men into the Hall and lay bedrolls on the floor of the Men's Room. But we'll need extra pads, stone's harder to lie on than hammocks.' She looked round. 'Fremtinc, go and get us twenty bales of bladder-weed stuffing. Don't talk about this illness—we may be wrong, and I don't want to look a fool or start a panic. Just say every pad in the House is saggy, which is true enough, and we're refilling them. Distom will see them about payment next tide. Dwymit, you know the store-rooms. Hunt up old sacks, curtains, cloaks, whatever you can find to make pad cases. We'll buy what we have to, but use the old stuff up first.'

She turned to her eldest daughter. 'Prentast, my dear. Fever powders and pain-stops from the Loops. Three sixties of people, a dozen doses each, that's . . . say forty sixties of doses. The Loops may not have so much, but buy all you can. And then, and not before, warn them about the disease, that they'll need to make more.'

'You don't think the Silvers will have told them already?' Prentastal asked. 'They may be rationing the medicines.'

Mother looked peeved. 'Maybe. Do your best for us. That's why I'm sending you and Crossten. Wear your best teeth, as many as you can carry, as if you're just showing off. Then you can pay for it at once, without alarming the City. Don't look so worried, my dear, everyone will think you're quarrelling already!' She smiled briefly, her eyes strained. 'They'll keep for years, if we don't need them. I hope we don't. But we may have only another tide or two before we're all ill. You know how frail Distom is, and we're all tired from the work for the Feast.'

Everyone was thinking, offering suggestions. 'The Triangle Houses might help—They should be warned anyway, they helped at the Feast—We'll isolate the children in the Nursery, and the Nurses too—At least there's enough food left over to feed us for ten tides, even if the yeast-vats are empty—I'll order another boat-load of ice, it won't help if we all get food poisoning—we can always eat the pets!'

A man warned, 'Bil has been in Silver House for tides. What if all the Doctors fall sick?'

Someone gasped hysterically, 'Oh, no!'

Mother slapped her, hard; 'Stop that! We can manage!' She made herself smile as the foolish one struggled for control. 'If I fall ill, I rely on you to run the House.'

Point Mother rely on them? They looked at her, and at each other. They all relied on her . . . But they'd not let her down.

At the new determination on their faces, Mother nodded satisfaction.

As Prentastal and Crosstenak reached the door, a small procession was hurrying along the terrace. The Doctor came first, beckoning Bil. The swarming Roof children who always seemed to be free to follow the Giant were tailing along beside Hemminal, who was keeping as far to the rear as she could, while still staying within what might just be called guarding range.

At the back, a big Silver was carrying Distom. Prentastal gasped, but the little man waved to reassure them. 'No, no, don't worry! I asked them to give me a lift to get home faster, that's all. I felt something was wrong. Chooker and Mungith—how are they?'

'Not well.' Prentastal was grim. 'Mother says she's never seen a fever come on as fast, or as hard. Mung was raving, and that upset Chook—you know how close she is to him. We've had to give her a sleep dose—it was either that or tie her down. You might be able to calm her.'

'We've got to get on.' Crosstenak took his new wife's hand. To cheer her, he grinned and rattled his festoons of teeth. 'We're going right up to Loop House, in all our glory. Let Prentast show off her handsome man!'

Prentastal snorted. 'Who's that, then? I only married you for your teeth!' She sobered suddenly. 'No, wait. Come back in for a minute. I need to hear what Bil has to say first.'

Hemminal stopped at the doorway. 'I'll wait here,' she grunted, and leaned against the wall outside.

Crosstenak winked to Prentastal. 'Could she be worried about catching it?' he whispered loudly. Hemminal scowled, but she couldn't think of a reply before they were out of earshot.

When Mother saw Bil stooping into the Sick Room, she scowled almost as deeply as the Kelp. 'Eh, eh!' the Silver scolded her. 'He's come to help!' Mother snorted, but stood aside and let Bil drop to a stool beside Mungith's bed.

Gently, he felt Mungith's pulse and flushed forehead, and nodded. He examined the young man's arms and chest and felt his neck, round under the jaw where some diseases made the glands swell. The Silver looked relieved; Bil knew something of medicine, at least. Then Bil acted wincing away, wrinkling his eyes; the Silver nodded. 'Eh, yes, light hurts his eyes.'

Bil nodded, looking happier. 'Floo,' he said. 'Floo.' He held out his wrist.

The Silver hesitated, but took it, and her eyes blanked. 'Ten tides, he thinks. Ten tides of fever, of floo, and then a long, slow recovery. A bad cough. Warm but not stuffy. Fever and pain-stop pills. Lots to drink.' She blinked awake and shook herself back to normal. 'Eh, yes. That's more or less what I thought. It is serious, but not fatal.'

'But what if this floo is more dangerous for us than for Giants?' Mother asked.

The Silver sighed. 'What more can we do, Mother Point? Though it's hard to believe, Father Silver says we are different icicles from the same drip. So we can hope that the floo will pass for us as easily as it does for them.'

It didn't. Within Bil's ten tides four thousand people, over half the City, were ill, including nearly everyone in Point House; and within thirty tides, over a thousand were dead.

Mungith and Chooker were lucky; they lived through the floo.

Mungith was ill for six tides, but then the fever broke and he began to recover. Chooker had it only slightly. As soon as Mungith started to feel better, so did she.

Point Mother fell ill on the fifth tide but refused to give in to it until the tenth, when she collapsed; then she tried to get back to work too soon, collapsed again in exhaustion and took two sixty-tides to get back to half her former energy. Distom caught the floo lightly, and soon recovered—he was tougher than he looked. Prentastal, who had no more than a sniffle, grimly took over and ran the dark-tide nursing, cooking, and care of the Family as Mother had organized it, while First Daughter Chooker was officially—with a lot of help—in charge of light-tide.

Fortunately, the experienced oldsters in Point House somehow spread out the floo, so that there were always just enough people fit enough to look after the rest. The Triangle Houses couldn't help; their members who had helped at the Feast, now remembered with loathing, had carried the sickness home. They had trouble enough to look after themselves.

The Coals, maybe because they were used to blocked noses, all recovered. The Houses who suffered least were, oddly, the Waves, who spent much of their time in the water and claimed that the salt saved them, and also those who had had nothing to do with the Giant. Tooth and Cavy and Fire Houses, and their off-shoots, cut themselves off immediately. They ordered their young Hunters to form their own boat-crews and hunt well apart from the rest, and forbade any contact with sick Houses except for charitably leaving food in the Roof lanes. They had some sickness, but avoided the worst of it.

In strong, well-run Houses, and among the sturdy Hunters, even though many caught it, most survived as Bil had said they would. All the Silvers caught the disease, but only four died, out of sixty—one was old Silver Father. However, the poorer, disorganized, ramshackle Roof Families suffered terribly. Most of them caught the floo, and barely a half lived. The Limpets and Stalactites, Boots and Felts all died, every one; Wilders had to be hired to carry the last bodies to the boats.

Nobody knew what happened in the Wilder Caves. Nobody ever did. They saw to their own affairs. No bodies ever came out, that anyone knew of.

109

But from the rest of the City the transport barges had to be used as Funeral Boats, to carry twenty or forty bodies at a time; men to Beliyyak's whirlpools, women to Fire Quay to start the trudge down past the forges to Bastiyyal in Fire Fall. The dolphins pulled the red-flagged boats up and down-tide, till the endless mourning misery made them unhappy and sulky. Finally, they stopped coming to the Waves' whistles, and the boats had to be paddled.

The Wilders earned a lot of teeth that dreadful sixty-tide.

In Point House nine people died: a baby; two young children; three old people; two who had been sick recently; and Crosstenak.

14

After fifteen tides of illness, when the epidemic was seen to be still spreading, the Council was called to an emergency meeting.

Chooker was kneading breads while Mungith picked the shells out of a cauldron of mussels. One of the older men came into the kitchen, shaking his head. 'He's mad,' he said, 'but you don't argue with a Father.'

'Distom? What's he doing?' old Dwymit asked.

'He told me to carry him down to the Council Meeting. Don't look so annoyed—I know, I know, he's still shaky, but he insisted. I thought you should know, First Daughter.'

'He's not well yet!' Chooker cried in dismay. 'He promised Prentast not to go!'

'That's why he went now, while she's sleeping. He said he had to defend the House.'

'Defend us?' Chooker was puzzled. 'Who from?'

'Defend me, he means.' Mungith's voice was bitter. 'For bringing the Giant into Atlantis. I should have killed it right away, even before the Coals got to us, instead of being so pleased with myself, so smug, so puffed-up!'

'Eh, stop dramatizing yourself!' Dwymit snapped at him. 'You're an Adult now, so stop acting like a child. Just get on with that soup. Claiming all the guilt is as sure a sign of conceit as taking all the praise.'

'But it's true,' he muttered. 'I've caused all this sickness, and Point House will be blamed, and lose respect, and it's my fault. And besides, this is a disaster. A health disaster. So this Council meeting must be to say that the Queen should die.'

Nobody had wanted to be the first to say it. It was Custom,

111

of course. If the Little Gods showed displeasure by sending disaster on Atlantis, the King or Queen, symbols of the people, must appease them. Beliyyak fed Atlantis; if the fish vanished, or disease hit the farms or the yeast-vats, the King must leap into Fire Fall, where his soul, unlike a woman's, would burn up and never be reborn. Bastiyyal cared more for the work of Atlantis, so any problem with the mines or people's health was hers. To pacify her, the Queen must throw herself into the Whirlies, to be lost forever in the black waters.

Chooker swallowed. Only about one King or Queen in ten actually ever had to make the sacrifice. But when the need came, if they showed any hesitation, Atlantis would suffer. It was probably the Queen herself who had summoned the Council.

Mungith was miserable. 'Why should the Queen die, when it's my fault? I did it. I thought I was so wonderful, and I killed all these people. Little Leed, and old Mistiom, and—' his voice cracked—'and Crossten. It was me. My fault.' Suddenly he shoved himself to his feet. 'I can't stay here and wait. I must know what's happening.'

'Don't be silly!' Chooker was alarmed. 'You'll find out soon enough. You can't go anyway, they only let Adults in to watch—'

'I'm an Adult! I've got to go! Even if it's only to say I'm sorry.' He headed for the door.

'Eh, sit down!' Chooker called after him, but he kept going. She made a face at the old woman beside her. 'Please, Dwymit, will you put these loaves in the oven for me? He's only been up for five days. He's not fit to go out yet, not into a crowd. I'll go and fetch him back.'

'Ay, ay, on you go, Chook.' Dwymit smiled wearily as Chooker ran to wash her hands and hurry out. 'They'll make a good couple, eh?' she asked the room in general. There was a nodding of heads all round.

Mungith was at the steps before Chooker reached the door. 'Oy! Stop, Mung!' she yelled. He just glanced back, and then sat down on the top of the children's slide and shoved off. 'Eh, Beliyyak take you!' she muttered. She had to take the steps, and although she hurried, by the time she caught him he was half-way down to the Royal House. He must be a good deal stronger than she had thought.

There was a considerable crowd in the street, in spite of the floo. Wrapped in her worry for Mungith, Chooker thought nothing of it until suddenly she caught the mumbling and thoughts surrounding her. 'Point—he's Point—it's him— he brought it in!' The faces around her were threatening. Voices rose to snarling, to shouting. Mungith was being jostled, more and more roughly. They were like the Giants; fists were even being shaken, in the street!

Terrified for him by the weight of malice and fear, Chooker pushed forward. 'What bad Manners!' she screeched. 'Like Wilders!' That worst of accusations made the crowd hesitate. Chooker looked for a way out. She had to get Mungith away fast. They couldn't turn back against the anger behind them. Forward, the door to the Royal House was blocked, jammed with people. What could they do?

Luckily, at that moment the Council horn sounded. All the Mothers and Fathers who were coming had arrived, and now ordinary people could fill the other seats in the big Council Room. The crowd turned back towards the doorway. The nearest shook fists at Mungith, but they were more interested in getting in.

Mungith tried to get in too, but they drove him back. 'Clear off! Haven't you done enough harm?' one woman hissed. Chooker pulled him off to one side, round a big rock, and up a path in the side of the outcrop in which the Royal House was dug. He was too shaken to object much.

The top of the rock was a favourite place for oldsters to watch the harbour from, but today it was clear. Chooker

113

helped Mungith to a seat. 'Eh, Mung, someone's hit you! Your nose is bleeding—here, I'll wipe it. You shouldn't have come out.'

'Shut up! I don't need you to tell me what not to do!' Mungith was panting in frustration and anger. He knocked away Chooker's hand as she tried to wipe the blood from his lips with a handful of moss. 'Leave me alone!'

She flung the moss at him. 'Eh, you shut up! It was you got us into this! Charging off like a dodo-hen defending her nest, when you can scarcely stand! Right into that crowd! If I hadn't pulled you out, they'd have . . . they'd have—' She didn't know what a crowd might do, when it was as scared and angry as that one. She didn't want to imagine, either. 'You did so need me! You need a Nurse all of your own! You're just as puffed-up as you said you were!'

She suddenly realized that he was trembling violently. He wasn't well yet, and he'd been scared—though he'd never admit it, of course. Look at him now, trying not to show his weakness! Feeling guilty and sore and wobbly, and not able to say so! Idiot! Her fury faded, and her shoulders sank. 'Eh, Mung!' She waited until he glanced up at her. 'Aren't you going to snap at me that your name's Mungithak?'

In spite of the way he felt, Mungith couldn't help his lips twitching. She wan't bad, Chooker; a pest at times, but on the whole not bad at all. He sniffed dolefully, and reached for the moss. It wasn't an apology, but it was as much as he could give, for now.

They sat quietly together for several minutes till they were both calmer. At last, Mungith leaned over to nudge Chooker's shoulder with his own. 'Sorry for popping like that,' he said.

'You can't help being daft as a dodo.' They exchanged tentative smiles. She was almost as embarrassed as he was. Adults—and he was an Adult, even if only by a few days—

Adults didn't often apologize to children. He'd make a good husband, when she was old enough.

She looked round. 'Three years ago—remember? We were up here, playing explorers. We climbed along the cliff face, and I almost fell and you held me. And then the ledge crumbled, and we both fell off. Lucky it was the harbour below!'

Mungith suddenly looked more alert. 'Yes, I do remember. And do you remember what we heard? Just before we fell?'

'Heard? I didn't hear anything except you yelling and me screaming!'

'Well, I did. There was a Council meeting that tide, and the sound of the horn blasted up through a hole in the rock, right into my ear. It made me jump, and my foot slipped, and that broke the edge of the ledge, and then it all went.'

He didn't need to say any more. Chooker knew what was in his mind. She was already turning to peer along the narrow crack. It ran right to the edge of the Royal House roof. 'A hole? Could we? Do you think the ledge is still there?'

Mungith grinned. 'Never know till we look, will we?'

Chooker bit her lip. He was still weak. She was First Daughter, she should stop him. But he was an Adult now, responsible for his own actions. And besides, it was exciting, a challenge, a way of cocking a snook at those bad-Mannered people down in the street. 'Let's try it!'

Before Mungith could argue she went first, slithering down to the end of the gully and peering round. 'Yes, there's still a bit of a path. And handholds. It's just . . . possible—' She vanished round the corner.

Mungith heaved himself after her. He was much bigger and heavier; he might not be able to manage. But he'd try.

True enough, there was a series of lips and juts along the steep rock face. Only a cockroach could call it a path, but Chooker was already a dozen steps along, clinging to chinks and crevices. 'Take care!' he called. He had forgotten how daring she could be.

115

She flashed him a grin over her shoulder. 'As if I wasn't going to! Watch that big stone there, it's slack, it won't hold your weight, you porpoise! Good handholds all along this crack. And at least once we're round the bulge here, if we fall we'll land in water.'

Gingerly Mungith followed her along the ridges and cracks. His knees felt rather unsteady, but he had to find out what was happening, now, not later. He didn't feel too bad, he told himself. One step, two, five—here was the loose stone; he kicked it, and it clattered away. It was cold, out here in the icy down-tide draughts; he shivered and forced himself on.

Further along, Chooker was quite enjoying herself. She hadn't had an adventure like this for a year! Light and wiry, she found holds easily; it wasn't really a hard climb. People had races up and down the rock, for bets. Why did nobody know about the hole to the Council Room? Probably nobody had been up here during a Council. Just her and Mungith, playing truant from lessons, and going round instead of up and down—

Screaming, a bird battered past her face!

She jumped back, startled—a foot slipped—

Her fingers clung . . .

She found foothold again. Eh, thanks to Bastiyyal!

The petrel had been roosting in a crack, a deep triangular hole leading down into the rock. As soon as her heart stopped banging fit to knock her off, Chooker cocked her head above the hole. Below her, someone was speaking.

Mungith inched along beside her. 'This is it, isn't it?' she whispered.

He looked round, settled his feet more safely, and nodded. 'I think so. Listen!' he whispered. 'That's the King's voice! This is it!'

116

15

'We honour your decision, Queen Sullival.' King Pyroonak's tone was solemn. 'You have advised Atlantis well for many years. We shall miss your kindness and wisdom.'

Less than half the Council were present, but they, and the people crowded into the upper rows of benches in the huge hall, murmured gently. They all regretted the loss of the gentle, sensible old Queen, but in this terrible situation, what else could they do?

'And what about the Giant?' Shark Father's tone was as sharp as the purple spikes on his head-dress. 'He brought this disease into our City. He must be killed. And that boy of Point's—he mustn't get off with it. It was his conceit, his carelessness—'

'We discussed this tides ago. Mungithak acted as I would expect any young man of sense and judgement to act.' Distom used a touch of mental pressure to cool the ranting, but that was as far as he could go. Now, instead of sending, he strained to open his mind to all the Council, letting them feel his sincerity. 'I'm not defending Mungithak because he's in my House, but because I think he was right. If a youngster on Trial from any other House had found the Giant, I hope that he, or she, would act as Mungith did, and bring it back to be examined. I remind you also that it wasn't his decision alone. One of the Coals objected, but all the others, and the Silver, all agreed. If there is blame, and I don't believe there is, they all share it.'

At the hole above, Mungith sighed gently. This was what Dwymit had said; but hearing Distom say it, in Council—and no one contradicting him—was far more of a relief. He smiled at Chooker, rather waveringly.

'So what do we do?' Shark Mother demanded. 'Let the monster freely bring more troubles to us? The Little Gods are clearly angry. Will the Queen's sacrifice appease them, or will new disasters appear? Will the lava rise to the upper caves, or the ice fill Atlantis, or the roof fall? It must be killed at once!'

From the rows of Councillors and spectators there was a clatter of applause. They had sat still for Distom, unwillingly seeing his argument as he defended his young man; but they were mostly hostile to the Giant. It had brought in the sickness. It must pay for it!

Copper Mother, one of the few who both approved of the Giant and had not caught the floo, rose to answer. 'Bil deeply regrets the harm he has brought to us,' she protested. 'He has tried to make up for it. Your little girl has missed the recent meetings with him, Point Father, but he has explained how to use coal to work iron, which we've never managed before. Many Houses have found uses for wheelses. The Giant has given us many new ideas.'

'New ideas!' Tooth Father's tone was vicious. 'How many lives must pay for each new idea? The old ideas have kept Atlantis alive and flourishing for cycles beyond counting! Atlantis is balanced delicately, like a plate on a knife-point. These novelties will push us off, make us fall and break!'

'But the knife-holder is having his elbow joggled,' Rope Father said. The Houses that made things, rather than farmed or bred them, were always readier to consider new ideas, and Rope Father was a very clever young man. 'These Giants Outside are curious, it seems, always seeking new things. They've begun to come closer to us than ever before, and they won't go away. Bil found us by accident. Others may do the same. We'll have to meet them some tide soon, whether we wish it or not. And if we have killed him, what will they think of us?'

The King's Family, still recovering from Battle wounds, had lost seven people from the floo, and would have to adopt out many of the children because there weren't enough Adults left to care for them. He loathed the Giant. 'But they must soon kill each other off altogether, with their terrible diseases and fighting.' He looked round, gathering support. 'They're too dangerous to us. I think we should kill the Giant now, break down the tunnels nearest the Outside, and wait. They may never find us at all. And if they do, we can say we know nothing about the Giant.'

'Eh?' Queen Sullival exclaimed. 'You mean say what is not true? Like Wilders?'

'They are only monsters!' King Pyroonak argued uneasily. 'We can't lie to each other, of course, but to Outsiders, for the good of Atlantis . . .' His voice trailed away.

Above, Mungith and Chooker couldn't see the Queen's contempt, but they could imagine it by the coldness of her voice. 'Honour and honesty depend on the person speaking, not the person spoken to. I am glad I shall not be here, to see Atlantis disgraced by its King telling lies.'

Chooker made a face of frustration. She agreed with the King—some of the way. But lying . . . That was disgusting, shameful.

Queen Sullival was not finished. 'These Outsiders—there is good in them. And they're powerful, although obviously stupid and bad-Mannered. We'd do better, I think, to go to meet them. Send a few Sensers to make contact, and watch carefully. If they try to attack us like killer rats, we're not helpless. Fire House can control the fires below us; Ice House can turn our tunnels into raging torrents; we can see clearly where they cannot, and we have more caves than they can ever find. We're safe enough, if we meet in friendship. They have cures for their own diseases that the Loops can use—and consider, they may catch diseases from us! We can trade with them, teach them. Bil's Manners are better already, after only a score of tides among real people. Other Giants can surely learn too. It would be cowardly to retreat, to close off the tunnels and hope they don't notice us.'

'Cowardly!' Controlling his insulted anger, Pyroonak glared at the old lady. 'Sullival, we all respect you, but that's . . . that's foolishness. Is it cowardly to run away from a lava flood?'

Tooth Father agreed. 'Would you go swimming out to a pack of hunting killer whales in the lagoon, to make friends? No, you'd stay well clear. That's just good sense!'

Shouting and arguments started all over the Council Room, and individual words were lost in the roar. Above, Chooker shook her head. 'I know how he feels. I want to get rid of the Giant—but not kill him—but I don't know what else. And I want to stay safe in the City here—but we'll meet the Giants some day—'

'Oh, come on, Chooker!' Mungith snorted. 'He's brought disaster—he must be killed! Or do you want to risk the whole City dying?'

'Huh! That's a change from twelve tides ago. You were all for him.'

'I was wrong! I admit it! I should never have— Listen, they're going quiet again!'

The new Silver Father had suggested, with all the power of his mind, that they should see what Bil had to say. Absolute silence fell.

Bil came into the Council Room reluctantly. His leg was almost healed, though he still needed support. In the centre of the floor, where the mosaic of a fire-flow erupting through a whirlpool called the Little Gods to watch closely, he braced himself on his crutches before the hostile faces.

Silver Father stepped forward and took Bil's wrist. Although his brain realized that Bil had not meant any harm, his heart felt sick when he touched the monster. However, this was his duty to Atlantis. He spoke aloud to help himself concentrate. 'Should we make contact with your people? And if so, how?' He stopped sending, and waited to hear and translate what Bil felt.

'Noh!' Bil shouted at them. 'Noh, noh!' Desperately he warned them to stay hidden. Think, he warned them, remember the sickness that he had already brought—and he hadn't meant them any harm at all. Remember what he had told them before!

The King, who had been frowning when Bil entered, was smiling now. He'd not expected support from here! 'You see?' he crowed. 'Even a Giant—the one who has brought us this disaster—he warns us to avoid Outside!'

'But will Outside avoid us?' Rope Father asked quietly.

'If they don't know we're here, how will they find us?' King Pyroonak countered. The question fell flat. They all knew the answer. An accident had happened once, and could again.

After a long, uneasy pause, Queen Sullival sighed and stood up. 'What you do is your decision. Mine is to go to Beliyyak. My head and bones are aching—I think I've got floo. And I'm old and weary. I'm glad to go. But I warn you.' She paused, and her voice was grim. 'You must not try to flee from Outside, or you'll meet it on its terms, not yours. Giants, it seems, are like wild rats; endlessly curious and greedy, clever and dangerous, but able to be tamed. Go to find them, and you'll be like Hunters, in charge of the meeting; hide away in corners like cockroaches, and they will find you. And you know what rats do to cockroaches.'

In the silence, she sighed. 'My last duty for Atlantis is to choose the next Queen. She must not be a Granite, like me, or a Kelp, like the King. She must not be married. She must have recently distinguished herself. If she was Adult, I would choose that Point child who risked her life to save her cousin; Chooker.'

Above, Chooker's jaw dropped. Mungith turned and stared at her. Chooker as Queen?

'But since she's too young, I ask the Council to appoint her sister, Prentastal, to be Queen after me. I know her; she's a fine person. Forty tides ago she saved a friend from a shark, diving in with just a knife, and never mentioned it, not even to her House. She's young, but she's been trained as Point First Daughter, and we all know Point Mother is an excellent manager.'

'A Point? Like that conceited brat Mungithak?' Shark Father grated. 'Should we reward the House that brought us disaster?'

Distom's voice was cool and calm. 'Is it a reward, to be Queen in such dangerous tides? I approve the Queen's choice. I knew nothing of the rescue of her friend, but I'm not surprised. While Point Mother is ill, it's Prentastal who is running the House—and doing well, in spite of mourning her husband of eight tides, who has just died. So she's free, and capable, even though she is young. She'll be sorely missed in Point House. But she'll make a fine Queen.'

There was no more discussion. Unless there was total opposition to her choice, a sacrificing Queen had the right to name her successor. Besides, no one could think of a suitable woman in their Houses who would take on the task and the risk. The Little Gods might demand a second sacrifice—it had been known. Although the Councillors didn't want Point to have so much extra influence in Atlantis, they all nodded reluctant agreement.

'The Funeral Boats are waiting.' Calmly, Queen Sullival turned to the door, and there was a soft bustle of movement as the Council rose to follow her.

Above, Chooker looked at her cousin's stiff, closed face. 'It's not my fault!' she protested. 'I didn't ask her to praise me!'

'No, no, of course not.' But Mungith wouldn't look at her. He knew he was being unfair, but he still resented it. This was worse than Chook being chosen as First Daughter.

122

Nobody had been criticizing him then, at the same time as applauding her. It didn't matter that he'd been saying the same thing about himself, and that he knew it was true; Shark Father blaming him, calling him conceited—that hurt, badly.

Chooker puffed. He was peeved; well, he'd get over it. Silly dodo! 'People's mood has changed. Come on down to the harbour to clap Farewell to the Queen,' she suggested.

Mungith didn't want to stay with her; he didn't want to be with anyone; he didn't want to be alone. His temper needed to vent itself. Something violent. Something drastic, and showy.

'Eh, Beliyyak!' he yelled, and shoved himself off from the cliff face.

'Mung!' Chooker screamed. 'Mung!' She watched, appalled, as her cousin plummeted down the face of the rocks—

But even in his temper and frustration, Mungith had made no mistake. He had leapt out far enough to splash into the deep water of the harbour below.

When his head bobbed up, and she saw that he was swimming safely, Chooker gasped in relief, and screeched after him, 'Stupid cavy! Giving me a shock like that!' How dared he?

Should she dive after him? He wasn't well yet; she should look after him—no, she shouldn't! He was the Adult, not her! He could look after himself! Even if she didn't land on his head—serve him right if she did!—her kilt would be ruined. Mungith could swim either way, round to the pier, to see the Funeral Boats leave, or back to the shore for the quickest way home. She didn't care. She'd go down to the harbour to honour the Queen.

16

Chooker trotted back to the street and joined the mass of people following the King and Queen towards the harbour, where two red-flagged funeral boats were waiting. In the doorway of the Royal House Bil was standing, looking uneasy. Behind him, Hemminal was glowering as usual. Bil lifted a hand to Chooker. She didn't want to speak to him; she waved to him to stay inside, and went on with the crowd; not as many as there had been for the Battle— eh, only about twenty tides ago! What a lot had happened since!

The old Priest of the Little Gods blew his horn for silence. King Pyroonak stood forward, and shouted, 'Beliyyak, hear us!' The crowd roared the repeat.

Queen Sullival, in a red funeral gown for her sacrifice, called, 'Bastiyyal! Hear us!'

'Bastiyyal, hear us!' everyone shouted.

'I hear!' echoed deeply from the far caves.

The murmur of, 'The Gods hear us!' was heartily relieved.

'There is a disaster in Atlantis,' King Pyroonak called. 'The Little Gods have allowed disease to spread among us. Queen Sullival has decided she must go to Them, to calm Their anger. Honour her, as I do!'

Respectful Farewell clapping, soft and gentle, the hiss of the Queen's name repeated over and over, 'Sullival... Sullival... Sullival,' and the mournful call of the ancient conch-shell horn, rolled out over the water. He and the Queen stepped into their boats, and those Councillors who felt able followed them. The Waves had managed to call half a dozen dolphins for this last trip, but it wasn't enough, and the stronger people in the crowd filled the benches to take the paddles, men for the King's boat, women in the Queen's. This wouldn't be left to Wilders.

Behind Chooker, a grumbling mutter grew to a roar. Were they after Mung again? Eh, no, it was Bil! He'd come out, maybe to follow her because she had waved to him, and the crowd were angry enough to forget good Manners. They were starting to stamp, like at the Battle; in a minute they'd be attacking him. What should she do? What could she do?

To Chooker's surprise, it was the King who saved Bil. He jumped up to balance on the gunwale of his boat, and waved for silence. 'Stop! Let the Giant through!' he yelled. 'Let him see what he has brought to us!' Sullenly, the crowd shoved Bil, and Hemminal behind him, to the edge of the quay beside Chooker. 'Come down!' King Pyroonak called, beckoning, his face hostile.

Queen Sullival stood up. 'It's not all his fault. Let him come with me,' she said firmly. She beckoned both Chooker and Bil down the steps to join her.

Hemminal started after them, but the King called to her, 'Come talk to me. If there's a man in the women's boat, I can take a woman in the men's one!' Hemminal jumped to join her brother.

In the Queen's boat, Bil picked up a paddle, automatically copying the women round him. This was their duty and privilege, and they hissed in offence. Bil hesitated, but Queen Sullival called, 'Yes, let him help,' and the moment passed. The woman behind Bil was Chooker's sister Motor. Chooker waved, but she did no more than nod in return.

From the pier, Mungith was watching sulkily. Why should Chooker go, and not him? He was already wet; as the King's boat passed him, he dived in and swam over. 'Hey!' he called. 'Need an extra paddler?' They lifted him aboard.

Chooker sat quietly beside the Queen, who gazed round as if trying to fix the colours of the caves in her mind to carry with her. At last she sighed, leaned back and glanced down at Chooker. 'You'll be next Point Mother, child.'

'Yes, Queen Sullival. May that tide be long in rising.'

'Good Manners. No more than I'd expect in Point First Daughter. Do as well as your mother has done, feather, and you'll do well.' Sullival's eyes sharpened, and her bony hand gripped Chooker's shoulder tightly. 'Warn your sister. A hard time is coming for Atlantis. I'm not a Senser, but sometimes I can feel the future, and I know. But with good judgement and good sense, and honour, I think . . . I hope . . .'

She didn't need to go on. Chooker knew what the old lady was thinking, why she had been called aboard. She could hear what wasn't said; what couldn't be said aloud. *The King is not reliable, not at a pinch. He'll do what is convenient for him, not what is right for Atlantis.* 'Yes, Queen Sullival, I'll tell Prentast.' The Queen smiled gently.

Chooker glanced back towards the King's boat, and suddenly felt a twitch at her mind. Mungith. He was there. She didn't know whether to be glad or sorry.

When the paddlers changed over, everyone avoided Bil. He looked so lonely that Chooker felt sorry for him. Rather reluctantly, disregarding the disapproval from her neighbours, she rose and edged through the crowd to the open space round him.

He smiled a welcome as she sat down beside him, gestured to the red flags, and made a down-swirling movement with one hand. Chooker nodded. Yes, he understood this was a Funeral Boat. But he was pointing to the Queen's red robe and head-dress, and looking puzzled.

Chooker took his hand and touched his mind. It was a hard idea to send, but she'd had a lot of practice recently, working with powerful Sensers; her own ability and control were developing. Bil's growing agitation proved that he understood. It served him right if he felt guilty!

He gripped her wrist anxiously, and started to tell her about tiny little things, too small to see, that caused disease. *It's not the Gods*, he insisted, *it's*—

Germs, Chooker agreed, and felt drearily insulted by his surprise. After being in Silver House for tides, too! He might not have been in their main Hall to see the big lenses, but every Doctor had a pocket one, and they had all examined him. And as for this 'not the Gods' idea—who did he think sent germs? Everyone knew they didn't affect the people the Little Gods favoured. Like Chooker herself, apparently, and Prentast.

Bil seemed really horrified about the Queen's sacrifice. He wouldn't stop arguing, until she shook him off and escaped to the Queen's side again. Even there she feared he might follow her, but as soon as he moved, Motoral stuck a paddle in his hand and shoved him on to a bench to get back to work. Good! Chooker exchanged a nod with her sister.

They were near Fire Lock, where a woman's funeral would normally turn aside from the main waterway, up towards the road past the furnaces to Fire Fall and the Death Gate road. The lock was open, and two women were paddling out one of the small message canoes. This was rather unexpected. There was very little work being done at the forges these days, just basic maintenance—Tooth House feeding the pack rats, and Fire House keeping the lava taps from sealing up too solidly.

One of the paddlers called, 'Is this Queen Sullival going to the Whirlies? Wait, please, let us say goodbye to her.' The King's boat had fallen quite a distance behind; this would let it catch up. The Queen's paddlers paused gratefully, letting their boat drift on in the tide, and reached over the gunwale to hold the canoe steady. As the women clambered aboard, Chooker moved aside to let them approach Queen Sullival's chair—and was suddenly thrust sideways to knock down several women, amid screams and yells of alarm.

When she managed to wriggle free, Chooker gasped in horror. Bil had snatched someone's long knife, grabbed the Queen and dragged her from her seat and over to the side. The only woman near enough to grab him hesitated, afraid he might use the knife on the Queen, who was like a child in his huge hands. He lifted her down into the canoe, swung his legs over and dropped beside her with a grunt of pain, slashed with the knife at the holding hands, and shoved clear. He seized one of the paddles tied to the canoe gunwales and struck out for the lock steps.

The Wave boatwoman was yelling, 'Get back to your places! Paddle!' Among the other women, Motoral was shouting and waving her knife, but she hated the water, she'd not go in. Not taking time to think, Chooker leapt up to the gunwale, poised a second to judge her direction, and dived in, a fast, shallow dive that should bring her up right beside the canoe.

In the air, she wondered what she'd do when she got there.

King Pyroonak and his sister were deep in talk, and Mungith was paddling, when the shouting rose from the boat in front. Everybody peered forward. A small canoe turned aside from the Queen's barge and headed unsteadily for the shore. It was the Giant who was paddling! And in front of him was the red glimmer of the Queen's Funeral robes!

The men started to shout as well, but they were all in place and their boat was already moving through the water. Hemminal yelled, 'Catch them! Dig deep!' The boat rapidly picked up speed, and the Wave steered to cut off the canoe.

The Giant glanced round, and redoubled his efforts. Although it was deep-laden with his weight, the light craft shot forward—and stopped, spun half round. Someone had surged up from the water beside it to drag at the side, trying to tip it over. Bil swung his paddle at the head in the water, and hit it with a sharp thud. He glanced round. The King's boat was charging towards him—but there was a swirl in the water, a triangular fin nosing curiously close... In spite of his own danger, he spared a few seconds to haul the swimmer aboard.

In front of Mungith someone yelled, 'It's that Point girl! Chooker!'

The surprise made Mungith miss his stroke. His paddle struck the next one, and a ripple of mis-strokes threw that side of the barge off for a few moments. 'Watch what you're doing, you fool!' Hemminal bellowed. While the barge wavered and slowed, the canoe got under way again, heading for the steps beside the lock gates.

Chooker! The Giant had hurt Chook! Mungith's heart hurt. His little Chook in danger—that monster—he'd kill it himself! He heaved on his paddle, keen to make up for his mistake. If Chooker was dead—she couldn't be—he'd never forgive himself, bringing her out to the Council meeting, and then sulking off like that—if it hadn't been for him—

A shout from the men on the bows; the canoe had reached the steps. Mungith lifted his head to look forward. The Giant had rolled out of the canoe on to the lower steps and was tugging Chooker and the Queen out too. His stolen knife gleamed as he forced them up before him, supporting each other. Then he stuck the knife in his kilt waistband, and reached down to pick up the light sealskin canoe with one hand. The paddles tied to its rim clattered as he dragged it painfully, but desperately fast, up the steps, using only one crutch. He hobbled up and along the lock side after the women, past the closed upper gates, and dropped the canoe into the water again. Then, just as the King's barge reached the steps below, Bil shoved the Queen into the canoe and tumbled in himself, dragging Chooker to kneel in front of him. The knife waved, Chooker picked up one of the paddles and Bil the other, and the canoe swept away from the bank before the first men leaping up the steps could catch them.

There was no footpath, and no one in a Funeral Boat

carried a bow or a harpoon. In any case, they mustn't risk the women. If the Queen died any other way than in the Whirlies, the Little Gods would be enraged and Atlantis could perish. Shouting furiously, the men could only watch as the canoe passed round the first bend of the winding cave, and out of sight.

'Bring the boat through!' King Pyroonak yelled. The big boat was already being hauled into the lock. Then the lower gates had to be closed, and the sluices opened to let water pour in to raise the boat, achingly slowly. It was almost low water, there was a good depth to fill.

By now the Queen's boat had arrived, but there was only room for one boat in the lock. They used the minutes while it filled to reorganize. The strongest people, especially the most recent Hunters, manned the King's boat. The other, carrying most of the Councillors, would follow as fast as it could.

Mungith begged to go in the first boat, Hunter or not. 'She's my cousin! And it's my responsibility!' he insisted, till at last Hemminal nodded.

'What does that monster think he's doing, kidnapping the Queen?' the King demanded.

'More important for now, where's he going?' Hemminal snarled. 'Never been along here, not that I know of.' She glared at Mungith. 'Have you told him about Death Gate, out past the forges?'

'Not me!' Alarmed, Mungith denied it. 'But the Sensers may have. But I think maybe . . .'

As Mungith hesitated, the King snapped, 'Well? Speak up!'

'Bil may have made a mistake, think that this is the way to where he came in. Coalmine Lock is off the same side of the main flow. If he's trying to get back out, he may not realize—'

'Eh, yes! Could be,' Hemminal agreed. 'So he's lost. And your cousin—she'll stop him, if she can?' Mungith nodded.

'Good girl! We'll catch them! There's the gate opening at last.' She jumped to the prow of the boat, and stared forward. 'No, they're out of sight.'

Everyone knew there were two more locks further up. Bil could drag the light canoe up past them, while the big boat would have to go through the locks. Each time, he would draw further ahead.

'Stop moping!' Hemminal yelled. 'Get those paddles digging! We'll get them! And then—' The tall woman hefted the axe that was always at her hand, grinning, vicious as a rat. Or a Wilder.

17

Chooker didn't notice the first lock at all, but while paddling along the first cave she slowly came to her senses again. She felt better after she was sick. Well, a bit better.

The Silver Healers had worked hard on Bil's leg. The bone was almost mended under its splint. He could put a little weight on it and hobble with a single crutch, but he couldn't walk yet. Chooker knew she could escape, swimming away or climbing up the cave wall while he was struggling in or out of the canoe at the locks. However, she'd have had to leave the Queen behind, and she would never do that. No, she had to stay.

The King would catch them. She clung to that thought. Mungith would find her, as she had found him. He would come.

Bil was sorry for what he was doing. Whenever they paused for a rest, he was desperate to apologize and explain, saying, 'Sawree, sawree,' over and over. *I don't want to hurt anybody, but I must rescue the Queen, take her Outside to safety. So, I need you to help paddle, and to lead us out.* 'Sawree, sawree!' It made sense, in a crazy, twisted, Giantish way.

To Chooker's surprise, the old Queen seemed almost to be enjoying her adventure. 'Bil doesn't want to hurt me, my dear,' she told Chooker brightly. 'All this waving a knife— what nonsense! I have to go with him, he's too strong, he could just pick me up and carry me. But Pyroonak will come to the rescue. And you say the Giant thinks he's rescuing me, too? By taking me Outside? Eh, eh! But why does he think I want to be rescued?'

'I don't know. I've told him you don't, Queen. But he thinks he knows best. He thinks we're all wrong, and he's right.'

'Such stupid conceit!' Sullival tutted. 'Eh, well, he's only a Giant!' She gestured at a delicate silver tracery of rills down one wall. 'I didn't expect a tour of these caves on my way out. It's years since I've seen Lace Falls. There's a grotto right under the waterfall, with beautiful green stalactites—it was my favourite picnic place when I was young. Eh, happy tides!'

Chooker really didn't have the energy to cope with reminiscences, as well as Giants. 'Should I head off into a side cave?' she wondered.

'Oh, no, dear! We don't know how far they are behind us. They could go right past. And I'm . . . I'm really too tired and ill to go much further.' Sullival sighed, looking ancient for a moment before she gathered her courage again. 'No, better stick to the straight way.'

'But what is the straight way? Bil thinks he's going to the coal mine where he fell in. He hasn't realized yet that these are the wrong caves. Should I lead him down to the forges and Fire Fall, or branch off up towards Death Gate?'

'H'm.' The Queen glanced back at Bil, sitting with his head in his hands in the stern of the canoe. 'We don't need to decide yet. It's the same road for most of the way. Just . . .' the Queen lifted her hands delicately in perplexity . . . 'just wait and see what he does when he realizes. He may simply stop, give up.'

'I doubt it.' Chooker sighed, easing her knees. She took a drink—it was fresh melt-water up here, not salt—and splashed some water on her face. The water was cool, not cold; they were near the lava flows. Her head had stopped bleeding, but felt as if it was splitting. 'He's a fighter, he doesn't give in.'

'Like you, feather.' The Queen nodded encouragement. 'You're determined. You'll be a good Mother, when your tide comes. And your sister's like you. She'll be a good Queen. She'll steady Pyroonak. I thought he'd do well—

he was really very brave, risked his life to save his friends, that's why he was chosen last year. But in Council he's foolish, listens to noisy people, not sensible ones, and then can't admit he's wrong. He can be as stubborn as . . . as Bil!'

Behind them, Bil straightened and called, 'Gohwon!' At his gesture forward, Chooker sighed, and picked up her paddle again. She just hoped Bil's leg hurt as fiercely as her head.

Round the next corner, the waterway ended at Foundry Quay. Bil groaned, and gestured wearily for Chooker to help the Queen out and up the steps. He heaved himself out of the canoe after them, and had to turn round to stand up.

For the first time, he turned his back on Chooker, but she felt too dizzy to grab a stone and try to stun him. She could see two or three of everything, gleaming in repeating outlines whenever she moved her head. Besides, if she had tried and failed, he'd have been angry.

Bil stared back along the cave. There was no sign of the following boats, but he must know they'd be coming as fast as they could. Although the locks would hold them back, on the water they could travel faster than the little canoe with its inexpert and unwilling paddlers. They couldn't be far behind.

The big man sank down on to the wall of one of the half-dozen rat pens. Behind him, the big animals came nosing over, bright-eyed and intelligent, to investigate the strangers. When the floo first struck, the forges shut down and the rats had had a rest from carrying in baskets of metal ores, and finished goods outwards. Now they were working almost as hard, carrying bodies to Fire Fall whenever the boats arrived from the City. Chooker glanced at their feeding troughs; nothing could stand up to two sixties of starving chest-high rats. But no, Tooth House was managing to keep them fed and cleaned, in spite of the floo.

She jumped as Bil took her wrist. *Where are we? I've gone wrong?* He felt her assent, and sighed in despair. 'Sawree,

134

sawree!' He kept saying that, as if it helped. *But I must go on. How can we get out, from here?*

Death Gate. Before she could control her mind it slipped in.

He snatched the thought, with an upsurge of fresh hope. *That's a way to the Outside? Along here? Yes, yes.* She was so tired, she let him see the steep, rocky road. She almost hoped he'd go along it and out—and good riddance! But he'd take the Queen—no, he mustn't do that! She strained to send, *It's far, and the Queen is tired, and your leg isn't mended yet—you'd never reach it on your crutch!*

He gathered determination, as the Queen had done earlier. He stared round, looking for help. The saddles for the rats were racked at one side; she felt him realize what they were, and look again at the rats. *No, these are pack rats,* she told him. But he knew better. The saddles were meant for baskets, certainly, but you could ride on them.

Warily, Bil opened the gate of the nearest pen. Twenty rats surged forward curiously and pushed out. He was clearly afraid of the big animals' claws and teeth, and shook his head in wonder when they just trotted over to the rack and nosed helpfully at their own saddles.

Although Chooker did her best to delay, the four biggest rats were quickly saddled. *Where are their head-straps?* Bil asked.

Head-straps? Chooker made a face at his picture of straps holding metal bars in the rats' mouths to control them. Disgusted, she explained, *Rats are clever. You tell them where to go, and they go.*

Bil was doubtful. He tied pack-ropes from one saddle to the next, so that the four chosen rats were fastened in a string. Puzzled, they tugged and scratched at the harness, but Bil had fastened the ropes firmly. Before the animals could get really upset, while they were still friendly, he lifted the Queen and set her astride on one.

Queen Sullival had ridden regularly as a Hunter and Quarrier, but that was many years ago. Now she was stiff and shaky. The rat felt her unsureness and started to sidle and fidget nervously. Chooker touched it gently, telling it, *Relax, accept, help, she is old, weak, unsteady. Be kind.* After a moment, although it was worried and not really happy, it calmed down.

Bil loaded an armful of blankets on to the third rat of the string. Blankets? For warmth when he got Outside. He was doing his best. He lifted Chooker to the back of the first rat of the four, and swung his bad leg over the back of the last. The big animal squealed in complaint before stiffening its back to take the weight. Bil had to lift his feet from the ground; if he had stood up, it could have walked out from under him. 'Gohwon!' he called, waving ahead.

Chooker took a grip of the big pack-ring at the front of the saddle, and urged her rat forward. What else could she do?

Once the rats were on the move they seemed happier, and settled into their usual fast scurry through the winding tunnel, its floor worn almost smooth by the passage over many cycles of sixties of sixties of feet and paws. Jolting along, Chooker realized that she couldn't speak to the rats, not while they were moving fast. She didn't need to deceive Bil at all; their mounts would simply head down along the main path to their normal first halt beside the forges, and he'd probably never notice the steep turn-off that led up to Death Gate.

After what seemed like hours to Chooker's aching head, the rats halted. Chooker opened her eyes and peered round. They had reached Big Hand Cave.

This cave was nearest to the lava flows which Fire House channelled and controlled for the Copper, Gold, and Point smelters and forges in the long side caves, high and narrow, the 'fingers'. The dry, hot walls rose sheer, carrying the scorching heat of the lava high above the workers' heads, up to the ice sheet above.

Big Hand Cave was one of the few places in Atlantis with shadows. There was no glow here; the light was an orange glare, reflected along the furthest tunnel, the 'thumb', by big silver mirrors at each bend, kept polished by a rub from every mourner who passed. For this was the way to Fire Fall.

The ridden rats looked round, to see where they were to go. Round them the other mounts, which all seemed to have come along too for the run, frisked away, exploring the empty forges, nosing for left-over crumbs.

The Queen was drooping, starting to slip; behind her, Bil stood up off his own rat and hobbled forward to catch her. Chooker slid off too, and ran back to the old lady's side.

Queen Sullival forced herself to sit up, leaning on Bil's shoulder, and spoke to Chooker. 'Take me on to Fire Fall.'

'But... you should go to the Whirlies—' Chooker started to protest.

'No!' The Queen's voice was faint, and she was white and trembling, but determined. 'I'd never reach the Whirlies.' She gasped for breath, at the end of her strength. 'Fire Fall. This must be what the Little Gods want. Or they'd have stopped us. If it isn't...' she sighed, a tiny, exhausted puff of breath... 'eh, it's all I can do. Your sister will have to... Fire Fall. Make him take me there. It's not too far. I hope.'

Chooker glared at Bil. Look what he had done now! Spoiling the Queen's sacrifice!

You didn't argue with a Queen. But she was terribly weak. Could she stay in the saddle alone? Chooker touched Sullival's rat, and pictured him carrying them both. *Can you do it?*

He switched his tail confidently. Two pictures came to his mind; one was of himself bounding easily, loaded with baskets piled high with bronzeware; the next was of a frail old lady and a child, light as empty baskets. He whiffled his whiskers in contempt. Chooker had to smile. She hadn't realized that rats could make jokes.

Without even looking at Bil, Chooker untied her own rat, so that the Queen's one was at the front. She led him forward beside a stone and climbed on to his back behind the saddle. Just behind her, she sensed Bil moving the blankets to the last rat, and mounting the third, which was fresher. She clasped Queen Sullival's thin, bony chest with her right arm, and reached round to the ring with her other hand. *Go on, but slowly, please!* she told the rat.

Steadily, carefully, he started again. She could feel that in spite of his boast the two of them were quite a load for him, but he moved smoothly, even stepping sideways under them if they started to sway. She had never realized just how helpful and intelligent rats could be.

At their normal final halt by the entrance to the end passage, the ridden rats wanted to stop. Chooker insisted, *No! Go on! Towards the light!* Reluctantly, they walked on down the crack, moving slower and slower till at last they refused to go any further. The mirrors showed the dazzling glare just round the next bend, the stink of sulphur was choking, and Chooker's hair was crisping in the flow of heat blasting over their heads. She could feel her mount, brave and willing though he was, trembling under her. *Danger!* he told her. *Danger ahead!*

Yes. She knew there was. She had never been here before, children didn't go to funerals, but everyone knew about it.

Behind her, Bil kicked his rat to make it move on. It stood still. He hit it with his crutch. It had never been hit before, and reacted in outrage, bucking and wriggling violently. Bil couldn't keep his seat; he fell off, with a cry of pain.

Chooker slid down, and helped the Queen to dismount. The old lady's legs wavered under her. Chooker just managed to help her to a seat cut beside the path before she collapsed.

As the rats scurried back up the tunnel, Bil struggled up and caught Chooker's hand. *Where are we?* his mind demanded. *How do we get out?*

He swung round at a shout from behind them. 'There they are!'

Above them, at the head of the slope, a party of riders were charging towards them, yelling in triumph, waving their knives, and hammers, and half-finished weapons from the forges. The King was there, and Hemminal, and Motor, and forty more. Chooker's heart bumped as she saw Mungith's head at the back of the crowd. They were rescued!

Or were they?

Sobbing, Bil grabbed the Queen's arm, tugged her to her feet, hauled her away from their pursuers. 'Oh, no! Stop, please stop!' she whispered. But he didn't. Chooker helped the old lady stumble beside the Giant as he lurched on along the passage, round the bend—to halt, rigid.

A blast of burning light, a bellow of flame; the passage ended as a cave-mouth in the side of a canyon. Opposite, a golden gush of lava poured out of the far cliff, belching heat and stink to the roof high above, splattering into a glowing pool of boiling rock below.

From the platform built on the very rim, there was no way forward, no way up or down or across; no way out, except down into the rage of Fire Fall.

What would Bil do now?

18

Queen Sullival sighed, almost in satisfaction. The Giant's hand released her arm, and she slumped on to Chooker's shoulder, trembling with weariness.

At last, at long last, Bil sagged too. As Hemminal led the Hunters charging down the slope behind them, the Giant drew his stolen knife from his waistband—and tossed it aside. He lurched forward right to the low wall at the edge of the drop. Chooker saw him, a black figure silhouetted against the glare, as if he was going to step right over. At that moment she didn't care. It might be the simplest way out of the whole nightmare.

But the Hunters dropped from their mounts and raced past her. 'Stop him! Get him before he pollutes the fire!' They seized Bil's arms and hauled him back, knocking him to the ground where he lay groaning, curled up to protect himself from the kicks and blows.

In a frenzy, Mungith was trying to wriggle through the crush to get at him, shouting and waving his knife. 'No, Mung! Stop!' Chooker screamed, but he didn't hear her.

Grinning triumphantly, Hemminal hefted her bronze axe high.

Just behind her, Chooker shrieked like a geyser blasting, and caught at her arm.

Instantly, without looking or caring, Hemminal struck at whoever had checked her. The axe blade brushed Chooker's hair. Hemminal lifted the axe again, and shoved forward.

'Wilder!' Queen Sullival was gasping in distress. 'Stop it! Stop!'

Chooker screamed with her. 'No! Stop!' The fear and horror and disgust in her mind she threw at them all, as hard as she could. *Don't do this, it's wrong, he's unarmed, wake up! Stop!*

Motoral, trampling Bil in the middle of the mob, blinked and came to her senses. She slapped Hemminal's face hard, to bring her back to sanity. Other Hunters caught the thought, shouted and shoved till the foremost attackers drew back.

Yelling, mindless in excitement, Mungith wriggled through the crush. His long knife stabbed at the Giant's side.

Motoral kicked his wrist, and the knife fell, unblooded, to clink on the stone. She dropped to her knees beside him, hissing, 'You'd stab an unarmed man? You disgrace to Point House!' His eyes cleared, and he sat gasping.

For a few minutes, no one knew what to do. There was a panting pause. Bil lay still, too scared and battered and disheartened to move. Many of the Hunters, some still weak after the floo, all exhausted by the chase and the fight, sat down to rest.

Motoral left Mungith and put an arm round Chooker's shoulders to support her. 'Well done, little sister!' she whispered gently.

Mungith stared at his knife. Chooker was safe. The Queen was shaking but unhurt. He had seen the Giant drop his knife, as he ran down the slope. Even Motoral, with her explosive temper, had seen it, and used no weapon. But he had still tried to kill, crazy as a Wilder...

He breathed deeply, trying not to vomit with shame and relief. He had hated the Giant before, for bringing the disease, and making him look a fool; now he could scarcely bear to look at the loathsome brute. Hurriedly, without meeting anyone's eyes, he picked up and sheathed his knife. 'Use it with courage and honour and good sense.' And he had nearly, so nearly...

Rubbing his knuckles, the King stepped carefully away from Bil to take the Queen's hand. 'You're not hurt? Thank the Little Gods! You rest, Sullival, while we deal with this—'

141

'No.' The old lady's voice was faint. 'No time. I must go now. Before I drop dead in the road here, for nothing.'

Appalled, he called for people to carry her back to the boats, but she lifted a weary hand. 'No, now, here...' Her voice trailed away, and she gestured feebly to Chooker to explain.

As everyone's eyes swung to her, Chooker gulped. Her head was spinning, and so sore! 'The Queen thinks the Little Gods want her to go into Fire Fall, not the Whirlies,' she whispered. 'Or they wouldn't have let Bil bring her all this way.' Did they understand? Apparently; one or two were nodding.

The Queen beckoned for Chooker to help her to her feet. The King offered a hand, but she shook her head, kindly, as if refusing a child, and tottered towards the mouth of the tunnel.

She paused by Bil's side where he slumped against the wall. He raised his eyes to her, like a scolded pet. She smiled, a tiny twitch of the lips, and reached out to touch his face gently. With an effort, she spoke as firmly as she could. 'Don't kill him. He isn't a bad person, just wrong.' She stared at King Pyroonak, and at Hemminal. 'Promise you won't kill him.'

'What do we do with him, then?' King Pyroonak protested. 'I'll not have him back in the City!' There was a growl of agreement from all round.

'He came from Outside,' the Queen stated. 'Promise me you'll send him back.'

'To tell the other Giants about us?' King Pyroonak objected.

'If the Little Gods wish it, yes.' The old lady insisted. 'Promise. I'll not go until you do.'

At last, the King nodded. 'No, I'll not kill him, I promise.'

'Nor order it!'

He gritted his teeth. 'Nor order it!'

'Thank you...' Queen Sullival sighed. She braced herself, let go of Chooker's supporting hands and turned towards the watchers. Bil whispered, 'Noh... noh!' but he could not move.

142

The low clapping of respect and farewell began.

King Pyroonak reached out to touch palms with his partner, his own eyes filling with tears. 'Farewell, Queen Sullival. Go safe to Bastiyyal, and if this is what the Little Gods want, return to us soon, in love. Farewell. May the Little Gods watch over you.'

'But not too closely,' the Queen whispered, smiling at him and at them all. She simply sat down on the low wall and tipped backwards over it, out of sight into Fire Fall.

There was no scream, no cry; no change, no slightest change, in the roar and glare of the lava hole. No one ran forward to peer over and see what happened.

Chooker sobbed on Motoral's shoulder. Many of the Hunters were weeping.

Pyroonak took off all his tassels of teeth and tossed them into the fire. Most of the others added more. Even Hemminal, with a grimace, took off a bracelet of seal teeth. Mungith didn't have any with him, and felt ashamed not to be able to show his respect, until without a glance Motoral handed him a string of teeth. He'd pay her back as soon as he could.

Then they turned to Bil.

Chooker could feel their hatred like a blast off the ice. Alarmed, she protested, 'You promised to let him go! You can't kill him—not without breaking your word!' Sullival had already, in public, accused the King of not being honourable.

After a few seconds, King Pyroonak nodded. 'Of course I'll not kill him. Nor order it. I'll send him Outside.' Chooker sank back in relief. 'But I'll not send him back out through the mines, either. He can go through Death Gate and take his chance.'

Chooker groaned in distress, but he was keeping his word, and the Hunters growled agreement. King Pyroonak smiled tightly. 'I wish nothing more to do with the Giant. Hemminal, I charge you to take him and put him out, as he deserves.'

Chooker didn't notice the significant glance between the King and his sister, and Hemminal's tiny nod.

She sighed; it was all right, perhaps. Bil came from Outside; maybe he could survive there. She reached over to touch Bil's hand. *You're going Outside,* she told him, trying to focus. *They'll let you go, Outside.* She was rewarded by a look of incredulous joy; then he lifted her hand, and before she could feel frightened in case he was going to bite it, he touched it gently with his lips, and laid it down again, smiling to her. She could feel his gratitude. 'Thankyoo,' he murmured. That must be how Giants said thanks; she tried to smile back through her tiredness.

There was a general movement to leave. To Chooker's dismay and humiliation, she found she couldn't walk. 'Help me, please, Motor,' she whispered.

'Don't worry, feather, I'll carry you!' Motoral reassured her, and picked her up easily.

King Pyroonak led the Hunters who didn't feel fit for the trip to Death Gate up the long slope towards Big Hand Cave. They called up their wandering rats, and mounted for the ride back to the boats. Chooker was settled in front of Motoral, held secure in her sister's strong arms. Slowly, in no hurry, the weary group set off along the track.

Glowering, the rest pulled the Giant to his feet, staggering, groaning in pain from his hurt leg and the beating. They whistled up one of the free rats and shoved him roughly on to its back.

Mungith rode after them. 'Go with the others, boy!' a man told him kindly.

'I'm an Adult!' Mungith protested. 'I've the right!'

'Eh, your decision. It's not pleasant, mind!'

Hemminal glanced round at them. 'Don't worry about the lad, Wheerain! Good blade, this one!' She slowed her rat to let Mungith catch up with her. 'Saw you, and that knife of yours!' she growled confidentially in Mungith's ear. 'Pity you were stopped—you'd have saved us a walk! Knew you were a likely one, a born leader, first time I set eyes on you. Stay by me, son. I'll teach you a trick or two they don't show you in the Nursery!'

Mungith bit his lip. He wasn't proud of his actions. But this big, strong woman was eyeing him with approval, and Mungith warmed to it in spite of himself. He didn't want to be a Wilder's friend. But she wasn't a Wilder any longer, and she was tough and clever, no denying it, and Motoral despised him, and . . . Mungith needed comforting praise just then. He urged his rat on to stay close to Hemminal.

Half-way along the passage out, a crack branched steeply upwards. After a few sixty-paces the rats scrambled down into a big cave, and the way beyond was wide and low. Every rock was eerily rounded, every angle a curve, worn smooth by water many sixty-cycles before, not by travel. The glow here was a dark red. Riding along it, Mungith started to feel that he was inside a body, with blood pulsing round him. A dying body, for the wind was chill after the heat of Fire Fall. He shivered with more than the cold.

Then the red began to brighten into a twilight. It was summer Outside, and light-tide; they turned four more corners, and their eyes flinched from a blast of brilliance.

Death Gate was a fall of ice, not fire. Above the slot of the cave mouth a shelf of ice jutted forward to hide it from the gaze of the Great God Rassiyyak as He flew across the world. Warm air from behind them melted the ice slightly; it flowed out and down all around in a sheet of icicles, a frozen waterfall. Through it glowed the terrible white light of Rassiyyak Himself, far brighter even than Fire Fall.

'Stop!' Hemminal called. They all dismounted, and she shoved through to the front. Bil was pushed forward right to the edge where he could look down.

The rock fell away from their feet in a smooth swooping curve, slippery with ice, over a bulge and out of sight.

Hunters had gone down on a rope many cycles before, and reported there was sea below, which in summer melted away the base of the ice-fall and in winter locked with it. A narrow ledge of rock ran along the foot of the cliff. If you slid down, even if you landed on the ledge, and didn't die in the fall, or shoot out too far or slip off into the water and get chilled to death or seized by a shark, there was no way back up the cliff. You could perhaps walk out over the frozen sea in black winter, but where could you go?

Hemminal took Bil's arm firmly. She was grinning. 'Death Gate, Giant! Any last wishes?'

'Eh, push him out and let's get back!' someone called, shivering. Most of the group nodded grimly, one or two grinned.

Bil stood towering over them, past tiredness, past cold, past fear. He looked numbly out into the ice-fall, resigned—

And suddenly, with no warning, Hemminal's axe swung to crunch against the side of his head.

They all jumped at the speed and viciousness of the blow. The Giant collapsed in a huge untidy heap at the top of the slide. Hemminal grunted with effort and pleasure, shoved the blade of the axe under the body and used the haft as a lever to heave it forward, on to the icy slope. It slithered away, limbs flying wide, fast and far enough to hit the fall of ice—

A tremendous crack, deafening, painfully loud. The ground shook.

Mungith froze in terror. Not another roof collapse, please, Bastiyyal . . .

Beyond Death Gate, the ice-fall was truly falling. Slowly, it seemed, in a crawling avalanche, it crushed down, splintering its icicles, splitting into a torrent of glittering crystals and flakes, blocks and splinters that tumbled roaring into the sea below.

146

And there flashed into view the terrifying width and depth and height of Outside, incredibly wide and deep and high, dazzling light, bleak and icy, huge piles of black rock and white ice, spread before the appalled Hunters exposed on the ledge in the cliff face.

Blinding, Rassiyyak hovered almost level with them, glaring directly at them, the first time anyone from Atlantis had seen Him face to face in cycles of cycles.

Death Gate was open to the eye of Rassiyyak.

The Hunters dropped to their faces in terror, wailing, praying heartily. Not too closely . . . please, not too closely . . .

147

19

The only sound was the wind whistling in from Outside, now that the curtain of ice was gone. The light was blinding. Nothing happened. No one burned up, no vast voice spoke to them...

Freezing cold...

Nothing... Nothing...

Rassiyyak stared...

Yes, the roof was blue, dazzling blue, and the sea out here a darker blue, not black and silver...

And so huge...

Nothing...

They were still alive... unharmed...

This had happened to him before, Mungith realized. When the roof fell—and the time when it didn't.

They'd all die if they stayed there. He had been at the rear of the group, still inside the tunnel, sheltered, less affected by the light, less frozen by fear and cold. He had to help.

Move! Yes, move!

'Rassiyyak!' he called. 'Please, if You are not angry, not too angry, let us go home!' A hand up to shade his half-shut eyes, he made himself crawl forward. 'Come back in here! Before Rassiyyak burns you! Hurry!' he whispered urgently. How well did Gods hear? 'Come on!'

Hemminal moved first. Suddenly, desperately, she jerked herself back into the shadow. The others followed her more slowly, shoved backwards, slid away, hoped not to be noticed, sweated in spite of the ice-chill. Mungith reached out to help Hemminal, draw her into the shelter of the tunnel. Shaking and gasping, she slapped his shoulder. 'Thanks. Thanks.' She wavered on, feeling along the wall towards the breath of warmth round the corners, while Mungith pulled others in and pushed them to safety. The last one was lying curled up, moaning helplessly. Mungith and another man shared a glance, bared their teeth in determination, and dashed right out into the God's sight to pick the man up bodily and carry him out of the light.

Safely round some corners, in the comforting, concealing darkness, they gathered again, rubbing their eyes, shivering, recovering. 'It's a sign,' one woman was babbling. 'A sign! You shouldn't have done it!'

'Pyroonak didn't want the Giant to go out. Not alive!' Hemminal snarled at them. 'No, he didn't order it, but I'm his sister, I knew. Did you want to risk it surviving, finding its way back safe to the rest, bringing more Giants? More diseases? No. Don't fool yourselves, you all wanted it dead. And this way I made sure. That's what the King wanted, what any sensible person wants.'

'It's not what Queen Sullival wanted,' one man protested.

'She was soft!' Hemminal sneered. As they bridled, she hastily amended that. 'Sweet and kind and brave, eh, nobody's saying different, but too gentle. This is a crisis! We had to be tough to save Atlantis. We had to make sure!' The big woman hefted her axe. 'Anyone think I was wrong? Me and the King?'

'But Rassiyyak is angry! Look!' The frightened woman, a white-skinned Granite, pointed to her arms which were turning an angry red. One or two of the rest, rubbing burning arms and shoulders and faces, nodded agreement.

Hemminal snarled at her. 'Stupid dodo! That's just from the cold wind Outside on your delicate Granite skin! If the Great God's angry, why didn't He kill me? I'm the one that did it! He looked at us for long enough. If the ice falling is a sign of anything, you cavy, it's that Rassiyyak approves of what we did! We did what the Great Gods wanted. Rassiyyak smashed the ice Himself, to hide the Giant's body, to help us.

The other Giants will never find the body now! Rassiyyak is watching over us—closely enough! We're safe. And we've saved Atlantis.'

Slowly, as they considered it, they began to nod.

Mungith was kneeling at the back rubbing a man's hands to bring life back into them. Hemminal pointed to him. 'And that lad saved us! Even me—I'm not ashamed to say it! I was as scared as anybody. If that boy—that man!—hadn't stirred me, called me to move, I'd have lain there till I froze. We all would. We owe him our lives.'

That gave them something else to think about. They smiled to Mungith. 'Yes—eh, he's a good lad!' One gave him a string of teeth, which started a general shower of rewards. Blushing, Mungith bowed his head and murmured thanks. Everyone began to recover.

When the chorus of gratitude died down Hemminal looked round, catching their eyes, challenging them. 'This is what happened. Rassiyyak cracked the ice, and it fell on top of Bil. The Gods showed they meant it to die. And this boy is a hero. It's true, isn't it? No need to mention the blow, in case it upsets people. So we say no more than that. Agreed?'

Yes. Some reluctantly, most willingly, all wanting to get it settled and get away, they agreed. Many of them had wanted the Giant dead, and would be enthusiastic, when they were warmer. Nobody cheered—they were still too shocked and cold. But they agreed.

Trudging back along the tunnel after the rats, which had naturally fled from the din, Mungith tried to sort out his feelings.

He had faced a God—a Great God. He was a hero. And rich—well, on the way to riches, with eight full strings of teeth already, three bracelets and several odd ones. How did he feel? Bone weary. Too much had happened, too fast. The floo, and then the rowing, the chase, and the final drama at Death Gate—he couldn't take it all in, not yet. But he was a hero. They all said so. Even Chooker would have to admit it.

Under the exhaustion, his heart was swelling with triumph.

The thunderous crack and boom of the breaking ice had echoed along the tunnels, even to Forge Quay. Alarmed by the noise, some people had gone off to find out what had happened. The rest, tired out with rowing or simply too much emotion, just waited.

Lying on a blanket in the Queen's boat, which had finally arrived, Chooker tossed restlessly. 'Bil . . . eh, Bil . . . Mung . . . Where's Mung?'

Motoral damped a cloth and wiped the little girl's forehead. 'It's all right, kitten,' she murmured. 'You're safe. You did very well. More than anybody could expect. You helped the Queen. Look, there they are. They're all back safe. It's over. It's all right.'

Silently the Hunters rode down the track, unsaddled and penned their mounts, and climbed into the boats, scooping a drink from the lake, cooling burning skin, not meeting anyone's eyes. Their faces were bleak; naturally enough. Death Gate was a fearsome place.

Her face and voice harshly triumphant, Hemminal told the agreed story, loud enough for both boats to hear. The other Hunters nodded assent.

The tension in the King's shoulders slackened in relief, and his head rose in righteous satisfaction before he congratulated Mungith. 'Well done . . . courage . . . presence of mind . . .' Mungith treasured the words of praise.

Someone called, 'Makes up for bringing the Giant in.'

Mungith's exultation deflated like a popped bladder. He felt furiously resentful. His moment of glory was spoiled.

When at last the King let him go, Mungith looked over at the Queen's boat. 'I'll go and see how Chooker is,' he said tentatively, not quite asking permission.

Hemminal grinned. 'Fine. But...gentle, isn't she?' Her tone said 'soft'. 'Don't upset her.'

Mungith made a doubtful face. 'She always knows if you're hiding something. Maybe not what, but that there is something.'

Her mouth twisted in not quite a sneer, Hemminal said, 'So tell her. Your choice.'

Mungith grimaced. He mustn't let Hemminal down, or the King. They knew best.

He didn't want to talk to Motoral, but she was there as he peered over the gunwale of the Queen's boat at his little cousin. 'Is she all right? How is she?'

'Tired,' Motoral told him. 'Calling for you. Come and speak to her. That'll calm her.'

Rather reluctantly, he climbed aboard. Motoral wasn't unfriendly. Maybe she wasn't the one who had spoken up. If whoever it was said anything else, or if Chooker started to criticize, he'd... he'd—

Chooker roused herself to smile up at him. At both of him—her sight was unsteady again. 'Did you let Bil go?' she whispered.

'Yes.' He found it hard to say it calmly.

She frowned. 'Unhurt?'

Mungith could feel Hemminal's eyes on his back. 'He's dead. Rassiyyak Himself cracked the ice and dropped it all on top of him. He can't be alive. And I'm glad! We've saved Atlantis!'

There was something wrong...but Chooker was too tired to think straight. She'd find out later. Poor Bil... She was sorry he was dead... Or was she maybe glad he was dead...? And he had had his chance, it was a Great God who had killed him... You can't argue with the Gods.

152

She finally let herself relax into sleep.

Motoral tucked the blanket round her sister. Mungith's attack with the knife was wrong, of course, but there had been no time to think, and he was just a youngster. And Hemminal said that at Death Gate he had faced the light of Rassiyyak Himself. Not bad, not bad at all. She turned to tell him so—but without a word he had dropped a string of teeth on the bench beside her and was already hurrying towards the other boat.

As Mungith climbed into the King's boat, Hemminal gave him a friendly punch on the shoulder. 'Kept it quiet? Good man!'

'Man'! 'Good man'! Mungith's battered self-esteem began to recover again.

Hemminal grinned at him. 'Some of us tough ones here are going to make up a crew, go Hunting together. Want to join?'

'Yes! Eh, yes!' Mungith's heart jumped. Hemminal would lead a hard-striking boat. He had to be a Hunter for a couple of years, anyway. This would keep him away from Chooker, and let him earn a pile of teeth—even heroes had to be rich, to win the best girls. 'Us tough ones'! He grinned, and slapped palms with Hemminal to seal the agreement.

By the time Chooker was Adult he'd have won enough teeth to court her. Hemminal and the King—and everybody there, including himself—had done what they had to, to save Atlantis. The Gods had approved it. They had done what was right. Hard, tough, but right. The Giant was gone. It was all over. Atlantis was safe.

In the other boat, Chooker slept peacefully. It was all over. Atlantis was safe.